SINK THE BISMARCK

SINK THE BISMARCK

Duncan Harding

Severn House Large Print
London & New York

This first large print edition published in Great Britain 2006 by
SEVERN HOUSE LARGE PRINT BOOKS LTD of
9-15 High Street, Sutton, Surrey, SM1 1DF.
First world regular print edition published 2001 by
Severn House Publishers, London and New York.
This first large print edition published in the USA 2007 by
SEVERN HOUSE PUBLISHERS INC., of
595 Madison Avenue, New York, NY 10022.

British Library Cataloguing in Publication Data

Harding, Duncan, 1926-
    Sink the Bismarck. - Large print ed.
    1. Bismarck (Battleship) - Fiction 2. Sea stories 3. Large
    type books
    I. Title
    823.9'14[F]

    ISBN-13: 9780727875655
    ISBN-10: 0727875655

Printed and bound in Great Britain by
MPG Books Ltd, Bodmin, Cornwall.

'War is not an adventure.
It is a disease. It is like typhus.'
Antoine de Saint-Exupéry, 1943

Letter to the Author

The 'Hollies' Nursing Home,
Collingwood

22nd June 2000,

Dear Mr. Harding,

I have read your book <u>Sink the Hood</u> (Severn House) with some interest.

I know it is based on fact, though appearing as a novel. I feel, therefore, that you will be interested in some additional factual detail, with regard to the ship the poor old <u>Hood</u> was chasing, the German battleship, the <u>Bismarck.</u>

Perhaps you would like to come up here from Portsmouth at your earliest convenience to discuss the matter with me. I am prepared to pay your fare - the standard rail fare to Reading, where you will have to change and take the bus. If you possess a motor car, I shall pay your mileage.

I should be pleased to receive an early reply.

Yours faithfully,

Horatio Savage
Vice-admiral, RN (ret)

P.S. Bring sandwiches: the food is terrible here. I am housebound and cannot take you out to lunch. Don't worry about the 'grog'; fortunately, I am well supplied. H.S.

P.P.S. See note on 'Gestapo Muller', me and <u>Bismarck.</u>

The Savage Statement

The place stank of piss.

As I got out of my old Renault, I could smell it right off. There was no mistaking the odour – that diseased brown piss of sick old folks. Mind you, the home looked attractive enough from the entrance. Tidy garden, heavy with tea roses, polished steps and a brass plate, which announced:

THE HOLLIES NURSING HOME
Prop. Mrs Hakewill-Smythe, SRN
Founded 1998
All Facilities

Still you could not miss the smell of piss. But then all such places stink like that, don't they?

I paused at the door, with its customary security buttons, and thought about the complexities of getting in and out of houses in the modern world. Anyone would think we permanently under siege. But then again perhaps we are. Hurriedly I swallowed the rest of my Polo mint. Perhaps it would remove the smell of the pint of beer I'd just imbibed at the local pub. I didn't want to offend 'Prop. Mrs Hakewill-Smythe, SRN', did I? At least *I* wasn't going to smell.

Then I tapped in the code. A click. The door swung open and I was able to see into the lobby.

The old ladies sitting there didn't turn. Instead they slumped in their stained Parker-Knolls, old hairy jaws quivering as they babbled with their toothless gums of some happier past world. Still they were sane enough to realise that they had to be near that outer door. Their crazy old, worn brains could still reason that it was their last link with the real world.

'The Prop.', Mrs Hakewill-Smythe SRN, received me personally. She was blonde and brassy. Her fat body was enclosed in an expensive blue silk frock *à la* Queen Mother, the shape of the corset below clearly revealed by the silk. She smiled warmly, all capped teeth – at the fees she charged she could afford them! – but her bright eyes were smart and calculating like a cash register. 'Ah! Mr Harding, the writer,' she gushed, taking my hand. Her accent was definitely *not* 'Mrs Hakewill-Smythe'; it was more 'Smith out of North London'. But she had learned the business. 'Mr Harding, the writer' showed that. She knew how to flatter the paying customers and their friends. 'Here to see the dear Admiral. I'll show you to his domicile myself.' She flashed a look at the slovenly care assistant in the cheap nylon apron, carrying a bedpan. The girl got the message. She disappeared instantly into the lavatory.

She took my hand, as if I were one of her patients and I could smell her discreet, but expensive perfume. Her fees *were* higher than most, so that she was able to afford such things, I told myself, as I listened to her professional chatter. 'We're very proud of the Admiral here, you know ... One of that bulldog breed who saved us back in 1940 when dear old Winnie knew we were fighting with our backs to the wall, eh, Mr Harding?'

I nodded. Mrs Hakewill-Smythe, if she'd have been alive then, I thought, would have probably been fighting her war on her back not against a wall. I doubted that very strongly.

'Mind you, our dear Admiral is still a bit of a rogue, Mr Harding. Typical old seadog with a wandering hand.' She gave her acquired silvery, middle-class laugh and added, 'But I hope you won't put that in when you write your article for the *Gazette*, will you, Mr Harding?'

'No,' I assured her, 'I won't put that in the

11

Gazette,' though what the *Gazette* was, I hadn't the foggiest idea.

We paused before one of the doors at the far end of the corridor, presumably reserved for the male residents of the 'Hollies'.

She knocked.

The response came immediately, as if whoever was in the room had been expecting a visit. 'Enter.' The voice was that of an old man, but it was alert and swift.

Mrs Hakewill-Smythe tugged her blue frock down more tightly at the rump, where it was riding up above the corset. She put on her professional smile and entered, 'Your visitor, the writer Mr Duncan Harding.' She spread out her right hand gracefully like a head waiter ushering a special guest, who tipped well, to a particularly good seat in a restaurant.

The Admiral – Vice-Admiral Horatio Savage, DSC, MC, to be exact, sat upright in his wheelchair and glared at the 'Prop'. 'All right. Thank you.' He held up a hand urging Mrs Hakewill-Smythe to stay put. Instead, though, she crossed the bare room, as if she wished to plump up his back cushion. 'I'm all right,' he snapped icily, and I could see that the crusty old bird had long seen through her. As he told me later, 'With that old trout, I lock up everything of value, Harding. God knows what she'll do with my stuff when I snuff it. But then it won't matter. I've got no one to leave it to after all, what?'

'Now,' he said when she asked if he needed anything, 'another bottle of grog for the two of us and have one of your skivvies clean out the commode, will you. It smells worse than a knocking shop in here. Thank you. You can go.'

Surprisingly enough the 'Prop', who looked as if she could be a real tartar under other circumstances, went, still giving the cranky old man with the hard angular face and square jaw her fake smile.

Five minutes later the two of us were sharing a bottle of 'grog', warm and without ice, which turned out to be the cheapest kind of rum from the local supermarket. The Vice-Admiral remarked, 'Real paint-stripper, Harding, but it puts a bit o' fire in an old fart like me, and makes a man forget this bloody prison and its bloody pong.'

I told myself, he was 'Savage' by name and savage by nature. I took another drink of that fearsome cheap rum, wondering how my guts could survive and waited, too, for his first reference to the letter he had sent me the previous week. It was that which had brought me to the 'Hollies', this smelly last resting place for the country's OAPs. But I guessed I would have to wait till the old boy

13

in the wheelchair was good and ready. Old and frail he might be, but Vice-Admiral Horatio Savage would want to stay in command until he no longer had the breath to command.

In the end, after we (read 'he') had consumed half a bottle of that dreadful firewater, the opening came from him, 'Well what do you think of my Gestapo Müller business and naturally its connection with the *Bismarck*?'

Unfortunately at that moment, I was just in the process of allowing the smallest possible amount of rum to pass down into my innards when his question caught me by surprise and started me off into a series of hacking coughs. He watched my face turn scarlet – eyes blinded by tears – with apparent surprise, saying, 'Weak as gnat's piss, really. Must have gone down the wrong hole. But keep it down to a dull roar, Harding – the coughing I mean – or they'll be in here like a flash with their bedpans and bloody down-boy pills. Well?'

In the end, I summoned up enough breath to wheeze, 'I ... I thought your letter very interesting and ... and ... quite a surprise.'

Vice-Admiral Savage smiled thinly, revealing that he still had his own teeth at least, and said, 'Thought the old boy was probably barmy too, I'll be bound. You asked yourself no doubt, when did they let that one out of the funny farm. What?' He laughed.

I didn't. I simply didn't have the strength. Instead, in an attempt to make conversation and prevent him from offering me some more of his 'gnat's piss,' I said, 'You must remember that my book – the one you referred to in your letter, Admiral – was fiction, or at the best faction. You know, a mixture of fact and fiction.'

He nodded, his hard blue eyes sizing me up, as if he was wondering whether I was the right type for what he wanted. Was I just what he would have undoubtedly called a 'bloody scribbler'?

'I understand, Harding. All the same I thought you did a good job on the poor old *Hood*, even if it was mostly fiction, as you point out.'

I liked that. Show me an author who wouldn't. So I said, 'That's kind of you, Admiral, and I must admit that I was intrigued about your reference to the head of the Gestapo – Heinrich Müller.'

'A hard-looking Hun bastard,' the Admiral said half to himself.

'And the fate of the German battleship *Bismarck*.' I paused and hoped he wouldn't reach for the Happy Islander rum again. 'I must confess to you, though, Admiral, it is a bit far-fetched. A Gestapo chief using you to help sink the *Bismarck*!'

'Stranger things have happened at sea, as they say, Harding. Besides after the war, Gestapo Müller disappeared. They caught all the rest, including that swine Eichmann, but not Müller. And as you probably know, he is still wanted as a war criminal, though he'd be a hundred years old now, if he were still alive.' He eyed the half-empty bottle significantly, and I shook my head hastily but the next moment wished I hadn't; I'd got a headache from the damned paint-stripper already. 'But naturally he had his reasons. Müller was working for the Reds, of course,' Savage continued. 'He thought the future lay in the Peasants' and Workers' Paradise, ha, ha and bugger old Hitler.'

Savage had one of the defects of old age. He was a bit garrulous and found it difficult to stick to the point. Still what he had to say was definitely interesting. It *would* give a new dimension to the old proud story of the sinking of the *Bismarck*. So I said, 'What exactly do you feel you could contribute to any retelling of the *Bismarck* saga, Admiral?'

Later I realised I had been a bit cruel to the old dog by behaving in that rather dogmatic, no-nonsense manner. Admiral Savage was not really interested in rewriting the history of a famous sea battle. His driving force was a more personal one: a question of betrayal

16

and counter-betrayal, a love won and a love lost. A point in time about which a person can say, 'Here my life changed irrevocably!'

Savage took his time. His eyes took on a faraway look. It was as if he were viewing scenes from long, long ago that only he could visualise. Then he said, 'Harding, I'd like to tell you my history so that it isn't lost for ever.'

Suddenly his bottom lip quivered. That worried me. It is a character weakness of mine, but I hate embarrassing, sentimental moments. He pulled himself together and went on, 'All the people I once knew are dead, you know, and once your friends are dead, you are dead too. Your memory vanishes with them.' He cleared his throat gruffly and this time I accepted his rum without demur.

With his wrinkled hand, covered with the brown liver spots of old age, he indicated his bedroom with its commode, spare bedpan and row after row of pillboxes on the dresser, as if the place said it all. He wanted to go out leaving behind more than that.

'So, Harding,' his voice picked up, 'write my story.' It wasn't a request; it was an order. I didn't know it then, but it would be the last order that Vice-Admiral Horatio Savage, DSC, MC would ever give...

17

BOOK ONE

The Savage Escape

One

'Time ... You ready to go?' The dispatcher hissed.

The young sub-lieutenant, his face ashen and glazed with sweat, nodded his head. Outside there was no sound save that of the steady tread of the sentry's steel-shod boots beyond the main gate. Naval POW camp Wesertimke Marlag was asleep. Or so it seemed.

The young naval officer grabbed his bundle, whispered hoarsely, 'The Navy's here, chaps,' and moved closer to the door. Behind him the rest of his stick did the same.

The officer next to the dispatcher, muffled up in a dark duffle coat, thrust the skeleton key carefully into the lock. It was made of a pilchard tin-opener. He grunted, testing the lock carefully. If the key broke, that would mean the end of three months' hard graft and short rations. 'Harry the Horse', the camp's senior naval officer, tensely gripped his unlit pipe between his big yellow teeth that gave him his nickname. His knuckles

21

whitened. Fervently, he prayed that the key would hold up.

It did. The old door opened with a rusty click. 'Good show, Mallory,' he said to the man with the key. 'All right, let's get this little show on the road, chaps.'

Now things started to move fast. The door was pushed open further. The days of secretly lubricating it with the oil from sardine cans paid off. It hardly made a sound, letting in a rush of icy-cold winter air. The senior naval officer shivered – and it wasn't just with cold.

Outside the blackout was perfect. Not a light showed. Even the drunks who had left the *Offizierskasino* an hour ago had been careful. They had turned everything off and checked the blackout curtains and shutters before staggering off into the night.

'*Number one – GO,*' the dispatcher hissed fervently.

'Good home run, Charley,' the others whispered. Then the young officer with the bundle was stumbling through the door and running at an awkward crouch. The rest of the stick caught one final glimpse of him, then the door was closed once more and all they could hear was the soft crunch of his boots, muffled with socks, flying across the hard surface of the frozen snow. The great escape from Wesertimke had commenced.

Now Harry the Horse began his countdown. The others hardly dared breathe. In the masked yellow light cast by the single electric bulb of the hut, the senior naval officer looked down the line of the escapers. They were all equally pale-faced, strained, tense, save one – Savage.

Lieutenant-Commander Horatio Savage's hard, emaciated face showed no emotion save bold impatient determination. Harry the Horse nodded, as if confirming something to himself. It was typical of the man. He never displayed his emotions. For Savage feelings were a weakness.

Harry the Horse's frown deepened even more. He wondered if he had done right in allowing Savage to go out with the first stick. He knew that Lieutenant-Commander Savage was a dangerous man. If anything went wrong, he had long realised, the younger man wouldn't hesitate to kill. He had been in the bag since his corvette had been sunk off Dunkirk the previous year and he had been eating his heart out ever since trying to get back into the war. Savage would now let nothing stop him in achieving that aim. He was not just escaping the boredom, the sexless stink of the fetid overcrowded huts, with their odour of piss buckets and human misery. Savage was escaping to fight once again come what may. That made him a dangerous man, a very dangerous one indeed.

The dispatcher went into action again now. Outside, all was silent. It was obvious the young officer had sneaked safely through the perimeter fence. Swiftly, one by one, with thirty second intervals between each man, the others of the stick slipped through the door and into the dangerous world of the Third Reich beyond. And no one really knew what the feared German secret police would do to an escaper: these Gestapo men were a law unto themselves.

Now the stick was almost through. It was Savage's turn. Harry the Horse cleared his throat. Although he outranked Savage by two rings, he always found it awkward, decidedly awkward, to talk to the man. 'Savage, I know you'll make a go of it if anyone can.'

Savage didn't respond. The senior naval officer thought, 'Damn your eyes, Savage, have the decency to look interested.' But Savage's mind was concentrated solely on the task ahead. Twice he'd been out and he'd suffered a beating and a month in the 'cooler' on bread and water for his pains. This time he'd sworn that he was never coming back. He knew that like an article of faith. Harry the Horse tried again. 'Do your best for the chaps when they're on the outside. They need all the help they can get,

Savage ... and you're an old hand at this lark,' his voice trailed away. The other man wasn't even listening.

Savage wasn't. He was looking for the last time at the squalor of the hut in which he had spent the last year of his life. His sharp, emaciated face wrinkled in disgust. Bearded, scruffy officers snoozing or reading books by the flickering light of candles. Others frying spam in homemade pans. A Canadian officer running a lighter down the seams of his dirty shirt, trying to kill the lice eggs hidden there. Losers – the lot of them.

They had already made their separate peace with the Huns. Now they'd sit out the war, with correspondence courses, amateur dramatics and, if they were fit enough, a little furtive groping of one another in the dirty stinking latrines. That was their war. They'd have precious little to tell their offspring about their role in the great conflict. But they'd survive for what it was worth.

'Ready, number eight.' The dispatcher's urgent whisper cut into his reverie.

Savage was wide awake, alert, ready to go in an instant. 'Ready,' he hissed back. 'OPEN.'

'In like Flynn,' the Canadian killing the lice quipped.

Savage shot him a nasty look. Next moment he was through the door, bundle over his shoulder, his right hand tightly gripping the homemade knife he'd placed in his tunic pocket. He was off.

Outside, he paused momentarily. Naturally he knew the vital importance of getting away swiftly, but as the Huns said, *Eile mit Weile* – hurry slowly. Never make any rash moves that might result in disaster. He grew accustomed to the darkness, covering the perimeter wire at the same time, moving his gaze from one stork-legged tower to the other. They were manned, of course. With a machine-gunner and searchlight operative. But there was no sign of the Huns. They had heard nothing. They were probably sheltering from the icy wind behind the wooden parapet, enjoying a crafty 'spit and a draw', as his matelots on the corvette had used to say before those damned Stukas had scuppered them at frigging Dunkirk.

All clear.

On the other side of the compound he could hear the faint sounds of the others making their way across the frozen snow and under the wire. There was no mistaking the twang of wire being cut. He grinned. It wasn't a pleasant sight. It wasn't intended to be. Savage knew that they were fools. Soon or later the Germans in the watch-towers would catch on. Then the 'Hitler saws', as the Hun guards called their lethal spandau machine guns, would burst into angry life. There wouldn't be many escapers who'd survive that first salvo. No, that wasn't a route he intended to go down, as desperate as he was to escape. No sir.

He darted forward once more. Crouched low, he crossed the snow like some menacing evil shadow. The stench of the latrines hit him in the face like a physical blow. There was nothing that smelled so terrible as an eighty-seater 'thunderbox'. He gasped involuntarily. But there was no turning back now. Time was of the essence.

Hurriedly, he worked himself down the corridor between the tightly packed stinking stalls. Here, promptly at eight hundred hours every dawn, a shift of four score men went in, paper in their hands and, gasping wretchedly, completed their task, with the impatient guards yelling all the time, *'Los ... los menschenkinder ... scheisse' doch schneller ... LOS!'*

He reached his own usual 'thunderbox'. In the camp, life was so routine and boring that people even picked their own 'bogs'. Quickly he dropped his bundle. He raised the wooden seat. Next he pulled out the stinking enamel bucket within, to reveal the dirty concrete floor below.

Hurriedly he swept away the dirt. He found the finger holes he had prepared

27

weeks before. He stuck his outstretched fingers into them like some old gaffer in white flannels playing bowls on an English summer lawn might do and grunted. The slab came up easily. Below there was a narrow tunnel and a current of cold, if foul, air emerged. Savage's harsh face relaxed momentarily into the suspicion of a grin. Everything was working out as he had planned. It had taken him three months of hard secret graft – even his fellow inmates, of the POW cage, weren't privy to this – to prepare his escape route. But it was worth it. Now he was completely on his own; no one else to take care of – worry about – save himself.

He dropped into the narrow pit with ease. His nostrils filled once more with the damp mildewed smell of the old, long disused sanitation tunnel. Somewhere beyond, in the darkness, he could hear the scampering of rats – the only creatures still alive in the place. To the end of his days, he told himself, as he prepared to move on, he'd never forget the claustrophobic horror of this place. Now he was kissing it goodbye.

On hands and knees, dragging his bundle behind him with a length of packing-case twine from the Red Cross parcels attached to his belt, he crawled down the pitch-black passage. For fifty yards, as he well knew, it ran slightly downwards. When it reached the edge of the line of thunderboxes, it would turn right. There it would be a little lighter. Perhaps there might even be a candle glowing, to guide him. He hoped there would. Hardly able to contain himself after so many months of waiting, he pushed on.

Scraping his head and shoulders against the edge of the tunnel – occasionally setting off heart-stopping showers of dirt that he prayed wouldn't turn into a major fall – he came closer and closer to his objective. Suddenly he swung round the bend – and stopped dead, heart beating furiously.

A great grey rat, standing on its hind legs, faced him, outlined in the flickering yellow light of a homemade candle. It was preening its whiskers, displaying wickedly sharp deadly teeth, staring at him fixedly, as if it intended to go for his face the very next instant.

Savage waited. He knew what was coming. It did. The rat left its perch. It sprang lightly on to his tense rigid body. The loathsome creature slithered the length of his head. He could have screamed out loud. But he didn't. Even underground, the guard, some fifty metres above, might hear him. The rat took its time. It crawled down his neck and slowly the length of his back. Finally it disappeared, leaving him sick and nauseous, ready to puke at a moment's notice.

He pulled himself together. With his right hand, now shaking like a leaf, he seized the candle that others had placed there for him – at a price naturally. Those Aussie bastards never did anything for a pom without a price. He pushed through the final soil wall and there he was 'Mad Dog Doogan', the Vanishing Aussie.

He grinned happily at the lieutenant-commander with his toothless gums. 'Hello, mate,' the big man said cheerfully, as if they met like this, in the middle of the night, all the time, 'doin' a walkabout, cobber?'

Savage was in no mood for happy chats. 'Shut it, you bloody Aussie madman. Couldn't you have got rid of that bloody rat? Frightened the life out of me!'

'Could have, mate. But I was saving it for my brekker. Make good tucker, rats do, if yer—'

'Let's not waste, time,' Savage said interrupting the easy-going Australian. 'You've got your pay. Let's see you start working, and get me out of this bloody place.'

'Right yer are. Off we go.'

Knowing that the pommy was in no mood for banter, the big Australian 'ghost', as his type were called, turned awkwardly and, then, like the half-rat that he had become, started back down his own tunnel, heading for the spot they had picked outside the perimeter wire, well away from where the other POWs, 'kriegies' were now going out.

Five minutes later the two of them were crouched outside the wire – shivering in the chill wind that came straight from the North Sea – eyeing the velvet sky studded with its remote unfeeling stars. Hastily Savage took his bearings. Next to him the Aussie was waiting – obviously for a tip of some kind.

'Where yer going now?' he asked finally when Savage didn't say anything.

'South,' Savage lied glibly. 'Heading for Holland and then through one of the networks that will take me to Spain.'

'Yer,' the Aussie said, spitting the words from his toothless mouth. 'That seems the best way. I'd take it.'

Inside Savage laughed hollowly and furtively searched his bag for a sock he had filled with damp earth. The Australian wouldn't lift a finger to escape. He'd sit it out till it was all over and go back to 'Oz', as he called his native country, to live off the state – and the beer he could 'win' with his tall tales of the 'big war'.

'Yer'll be off, cobber?' the Australian asked. There was a wheedling tone in his voice now. Savage thought he sounded like a cheap waiter hovering around his customers for a tip. 'I'll pray for you this night when I get back to my hidey-hole.'

'That's decent of you,' Savage said, irony in his voice, but he knew irony was wasted on the other man. 'I certainly do appreciate all you've done for me over the last weeks.' He fumbled inside his bag as if he were searching for some goodie to give the Australian.

'Think nothing of it, cobber. You might not be an Aussie, but you're a good bloke and we are comrades-in-arms after all, though you are—'

His sentence came to an abrupt end as Savage hit him hard right in the centre of the forehead with the sand-filled sock. Without a single sound, the Australian 'ghost' reeled back into the hole from which they had just emerged.

Savage laughed harshly. 'See yer down under after the war, cobber,' he snarled, with a poor imitation of the man's Australian accent. Then he was going, heading for the snow-heavy woods beyond the camp. He was out ... out ... OUT!

Two

The Tommy bomber was dying in the sky! Its starboard engine was shattered, greedy little blue flames licking about the still prop. Its port engine was going full out, as the pilot desperately tried to keep the English bomber in the sky. Below the fleet at Wilhelmshaven mercilessly peppered the sky around it with flak. The spy plane was not going to escape, the *Kriegsmarine* was going to see to that. Black puffs of smoke exploded all around it. Tracer – red, green and yellow – zipped back and forth lethally. Even at that height, the two observers on the quay could see the shreds of gleaming metal, ripped off the stricken plane, floating down to the sea like frozen silver leaves.

Fregattenkapitan Feuchtner grinned, without malice. Indeed he felt sorry for the lone Tommy pilot who had braved the anchorage of the German fleet so boldly – and so foolishly. 'He ain't got a chance in hell, *Standartenführer*,' he said to his undersized companion, apparently in no way awed by the presence of one of the most feared men in the Third Reich.

Gestapo Müller, small, shaven-headed and insignificant, even in the smart uniform of a senior Gestapo official, nodded a little nervously. He wasn't afraid, of course. He'd been a bomber pilot in the old war himself; he knew the drill. But he didn't like the sea and the people who sailed it. These men from the north of Germany were all 'sow Prussians' – and communist to boot. The coast, the sea and the sailors always made him feel uneasy; he was always happy back in his native mountainous Bavaria. 'He's trying to feather the other prop,' he began to explain to his naval escort, but broke off abruptly.

Suddenly the cadence of the remaining engine had changed to a despairing whine. He knew what that meant. The pilot had failed. He had! The nose tilted down. Thick black smoke started to pour from the 'good' engine. She was preparing for her last dive – to her doom.

'There she frigging well goes,' the young lieutenant-commander yelled exuberantly.

Now the Wellington seemed to stand on its nose momentarily. Suddenly, startingly, a sheet of flame seared the length of the plane like that of a gigantic blowtorch. A wing fell off and came twirling to the waves below.

Then, after what seemed an eternity but might only have been a second, it fell out of the sky like a stone. Next instant it had plunged into the winter sea. Wild white foaming water erupted in a furious geyser. A mushroom of steam shot up. A second later, all that marked the passing of the Tommy bomber was a swirl of oil spreading steadily across the anchorage, on and on until eternity.

Fregattenkapitan Feuchtner crossed himself in mock modesty.

Gestapo Müller frowned. Once he had been a fervent Catholic in his native Munich; he still didn't like that sort of ungodliness.

Feuchtner saw the look on the Gestapo boss's face and it wasn't very pleasant. Hastily he said, 'He deserved it, but I wished the pilot well – on the other side, *Standartenführer*.'

Gestapo Müller did not seem to be listening to his explanation. Instead he said, 'Is it always like this here in Wilhelmshaven?'

Feuchtner nodded and wondered why their guest had asked such a question. After all, he supposed that the Gestapo chief was only at this remote northern naval base – so far away from the Berlin Secret Police HQ – by chance. 'Yes,' he answered almost casually, 'the Tommies try to keep a permanent eye on our surface fleet. They can't do much about Admiral Doenitz's U-boats.' He meant the admiral who commanded Germany's deadly underwater fleet, which had already brought the damned Tommies almost down to their knees. 'But they can do a lot about our surface ships. Once they are spotted by the Tommies heaving anchor, there'd be all hell to pay on the other side of the pond. The Tommies would pull out all the stops.'

Gestapo Müller's heavy-jawed face, with those curious, shifting eyes of his, which made even the hard boiled lieutenant-commander feel a little uneasy, revealed nothing. He nodded carefully, as if he were storing up the information he had just received for further use.

Feuchtner gave a little shrug. It was no skin off his nose, was it? He'd probably never see the Gestapo chief ever again after this day. Not that he wanted to do anyway. 'The Tommies might not be too bright in the upper storey, Standartenführer, but they're damned persistent, that's for sure.' He tugged his tie into place above the Knight's Cross of which he was so proud. 'I suppose, sir, we'd better move off. The Grand Admiral frowns upon lateness, sir.'

'Yes, of course,' Gestapo Müller agreed easily. At the back of his shaven head, a malicious little voice sneered, 'Who in three devils' name gives a shit about the – er – Grand Admiral?' And of course, Gestapo Müller was right. In his profession, nothing or nobody counted. He only needed to snap his fingers and the most important people in the land would disappear without trace...

'*Stillgestanden.*'

The big open shed echoed and re-echoed with that tremendous command bellowed through the public address system. One hundred pairs of boots stamped to attention as one. The seagulls, disturbed in their roosts, flew away cawing in hoarse protest. Ourside the naval sentries paused momentarily in their beat and then carried on, sealing the shed off from big ears. Müller nodded his approval. At least these sow Prussians knew how to maintain security. The thought pleased him. It made his life easier. He relaxed a little, that is as much as he ever did. On the dais, fringed with the black and white iron-crossed flags of the old Imperial Navy, Grand Admiral Raeder waited before saying in his soft, old man's voice, 'Gentlemen, stand at ease – please.'

There was the usual outbreak of coughing, shuffling of feet, clearing of throats and indeed the barely concealed noise of officers breaking wind. Gestapo Müller's face took on a momentary look of scorn. Ex-NCO that he was, he had never lost his contempt for these officers and gentlemen – 'monocle Fritzes,' as his fellow ex-NCO, Adolf Hitler called them. Just like any ordinary mortal, he told himself, *they* didn't shit through the ribs either.

Raeder cleared his throat. In a reedy voice that went with his old-fashioned sword and wing-collar, he announced, 'Comrades, I don't need to tell you that our friends in the Army and Air Force have achieved tremendous successes in the last few months. The press and radio have been full of their exploits. Perhaps too much so,' he allowed himself a tight-lipped smirk.

Next to Gestapo Müller and Feuchtner, a young officer whispered, 'As long as the damned Navy runs on wheels it'll never hit the headlines.' Feuchtner laughed softly as he recognised the old pun on Raeder's name and the surface fleet.

'But I think the time has come, gentlemen,' Raeder continued, 'for you, officers of the fleet, to share some of that glory. Most of Admiral Doenitz's young men have already cured their throatache,' he meant won the Knight's Cross of the Iron Cross, the decoration which was worn around the neck and throat, 'and I feel that some of *you* should be cured from that same affliction – *soon!*' He beamed at his assembled officers.

It was a look which was returned with

enthusiasm. The U-boat officers had become like film stars in these last few months after their tremendous victories against the Tommies in the North Atlantic. It was said that they could have any woman they wished; even titled ladies offered them their bodies – by post. It was a status which many of those present this cold morning in Wilhelmshaven would have liked to achieve, too.

'What of the surface navy, people are asking,' Raeder continued. 'What role have the big ships played in the war thus far, the man-in-the-street demands. As far as the average folk – comrade – goes, gentlemen, they think we are sitting on our fat blue bottoms doing exactly – *nothing*!'

Gestapo Müller listened carefully. He noted Raeder's points, realising, although he knew little of the subject, that the old Admiral was jealous of the success of the much younger Doenitz and his U-boats. For Doenitz, who had the Führer's ear, was the future. He, Raeder, was the past.

As Müller listened, he wasn't quite clear to what use he could put the information he was now gaining, but somehow he realised he would eventually profit from it. For the time being, however, he was here to check the security of the surface fleet and its anchorage in Wilhelmshaven.

'Naturally,' Raeder concluded five minutes later, 'I don't want to discuss operations here and now, comrades. It would hardly be the place to do so. But I can assure you that they are in full swing. Suffice to say,' he paused significantly, as if to let his listeners know that what he was about to say was the reason for his coming here from his Berlin HQ to talk to them on this cold overcast day, 'you can confidently anticipate that you will be engaged in ops before the winter is over. And they won't be low-key, you may be sure of that. The day of the surface fleet is nigh.' He raised his liver-spotted old hand to the gold-braided cap – automatically Müller, the long-time cop noted the hand shook – as if saluting them. 'Comrades, I already wish you good hunting.' And with that the pep talk was over. The loudspeakers boomed. The officers sprang to attention. A little wearily, assisted by his gold-braided adjutants, the Grand Admiral descended from the dais and the air was abruptly filled with the brass-heavy bombastic march so popular that year. *'Wir fahren gegen Enger-land...'*

Müller frowned. One should never count one's chickens before they hatched, he told himself. Next moment he dismissed the thought as Feuchtner took his arm in that happy-go-lucky manner of his, saying, 'The Grand Admiral's having a piss-up. Might as well get the free sauce, *"Standartenführer,"* eh?'

The *Standartenführer* allowed himself to be persuaded...

'Lieber Herr Standartenführer,' Raeder said affably, using the wrong form of address for an SS officer, which made Müller think that the old shit might have been overindulging, 'how good of you to come.'

Müller mumbled something and wished he had a good glass of Munich beer in his hand instead of the champagne piss these officers and gents were drinking, bringing up their glass to the third button of their tunics, as regulations prescribed, clicking their heels and toasting each other.

'You've checked out the situation thoroughly, I mean the security business?'

'My people have, *Herr Grossadmiral,'* Müller corrected him.

'And?'

'On the whole, good. There are a few weaknesses, but I am sure that we can take care of them without too much difficulty. There are still plenty of communists in our northern ports.'

'Damned red swine. Should have shot the lot of 'em back in '33 when the Führer first took control,' Raeder said hotly, cheeks flushing, as if the presence of potential communist spies and saboteurs was a personal affront. 'Thank God, with your recent experience of the Red Orchestra traitors, *Standartenführer*, you know how to deal with vermin of that nature.'

For some reason that Feuchtner, who was standing close by, couldn't fathom, Müller's sallow brooding face flushed for an instance.

'Yes, I suppose so,' Müller said, a little grudgingly. 'But is there, Grand Admiral, something that I ought to know in addition?' He had long sensed, ever since he had arrived at this particular Prussian arsehole-of-the-world from Berlin, that he hadn't been told everything.

Raeder hesistated.

A naval steward, the back of his white jacket now soaked black with sweat, clicked his heels and presented his silver tray laden with flutes of French champagne. *'Champus, Herr Grossadmiral?'*

Impatiently Raeder waved him away. He flashed a look to left and right like a man who saw danger in every shadow. 'Yes. I suppose there is, Müller. That is why the Führer himself asked me to request your expert services.'

Müller forced his face not to reveal his contempt at the statement. All of them, even commanders-in-chief like Raeder, could not refrain from showing off with the Führer's shitting name. It was a kind of magic key, they thought, which would open all doors. But one day even Hitler would have his downfall. Then no one would dare boast that he had had the approval of the Führer for his undertakings, whatever they were.

'You see, Müller, we are going to start our own blitzkrieg on the sea. We have waited long enough. I know we are not ready, but one can never be fully ready – *ever*. If we don't do something soon, the Führer will lose patience with us completely. He'll have the surface fleet mothballed and leave the war at sea to Doenitz's U-boats and that will be the end of the real German Navy.'

Müller nodded in that wooden cop's fashion of his, his broad peasant face revealing nothing. In fact his mind was racing electrically. He had just been informed of a great secret, one that might affect the whole future course of the war. He had suspected all along that he had been called here for more than a routine security check-up. Now he knew he was right. Security was only a factor in the great plan soon to be put into operation.

Raeder must have been feeling his *'champus'*, for he added in an excited whisper, 'They're all going out – the *Prinz Eugen* ... the *Bismarck* ... the *Tirpitz*, perhaps even the *Scharnhorst*, if we can get her seaworthy in time.' The Grand Admiral's raddled old face glowed suddenly with almost youthful enthusiasm. 'It is nearly a quarter of a century now,' he continued, 'since the terrible ignominy of Scapa Flow. Now the time has come for the German Navy to take its revenge. This time the Tommies will pay the butcher's bill in the blood of their sailors.' He paused, chest heaving as if he had just run a race, staring hard at the policeman.

Müller opened his mouth, as if to ask another question, as cops always did. They never grew sick of asking questions. But he wasn't fated to ask that overwhelming question which would have made life a lot easier for him later. Instead a tall, burly civilian elbowed his way past Feuchtner, almost making him drop his glass of champagne, and hissed to Müller, 'Chief, I've got an important message for ... straight from HQ.'

Raeder looked angrily at the civilian, who had Gestapo written all over him, from his cheap cigar (unlit) to his mouthful of gold teeth and ankle-length creaking leather coat. The civilian stared him out. He was 'Secret State Police' wasn't he? The brass didn't impress him. He was a law unto himself.

Müller forgot Raeder immediately. Again, in the fashion of cops, he took his aide and steered him out of earshot and, when he was sure that there was no one listening, snapped, '*Los ... raus mit der Sprache.*'

The aide didn't waste any time. 'Top priority call from Berlin, *Standartenführer*. Officer courier only. The—'

'Yes, yes,' Müller cut him impatiently. 'Forget the crap. Where's the fire?'

'Everywhere, sir. Over half a hundred Tommy POWs have escaped from Wesertimke. Just down the road from Wilhelmshaven. The Führer's hit the ceiling. You've got to get them back *now*.'

'Then?'

The other cop stuck out a forefinger like a hairy pork sausage and jerked it back and forth, as if he were pulling the trigger of a pistol. '*That!*'

Three

The sudden shriek of the siren woke Savage with a start. It was muted a little by the thick wooden wall of the barge's hold, but it was there all right. The escaper shook his head – hard. Yes, he wasn't dreaming. It was a siren all right and the shriek it made was accompanied by the steady, but urgent throb of engines. A second later, he realised he was in trouble by the metallically distorted command. '*Achtung ... Achtung ... Wasserschutzpolizei!*'

'Blast and bloody damn,' he cursed, his heart missing a beat. It was the Hun river police.

Swiftly he squirmed out of his makeshift burrow beyond the pile of metal scrap for Hamburg's factories and clambered towards the hatch cover. Gingerly, he opened it and peered out.

A fat slattern of a woman in a man's sailor cap and boots was standing there, hands on hips, staring down at what he guessed would be the police launch below. By the look on the woman's fat face, he could guess, the cops weren't particularly welcome. He knew why. There'd be contraband aboard bound for the great port's black market. Next moment, he heard the heavy clatter of sea-boots mounting the ladder fixed to the side of the Elbe barge and knew that the police were coming aboard to search the ancient craft.

Savage cast a quick look to the opposite bank of the great river away from the still hidden police launch. There, the sandy bank was covered in dense firs, their tops still wreathed in a powder of white snow. It would provide an excellent place to hide. But he'd never make it. The police, still on the launch, would undoubtedly spot the swimmer before he got that far. If he was going to make a break for it, it had to be the nearside bank. But there was still that little runt – he guessed he was the slattern woman's lover or husband. He'd spot him going over the side and shout to the men in the police launch below. It would be an obvious tactic in order to take the pressure off him and prevent the cops from searching for the barge's hidden black market wares.

Savage bit his bottom lip. What was he going to do? He hadn't come this far to get caught now. Somehow, he would have to cause a diversion and do a swift bunk while the cops were occupied elsewhere. But what? Then he had it.

Gingerly he dropped back into the open hold. He picked up the two precious packets of camp tobacco; that was his currency, the way he'd buy himself aboard a neutral Swedish freighter at Lubeck, as was his plan. He reached the deck again. In that same instant a big red-faced policeman came over the side, pistol held in his free hand.

Savage knew why immediately. They weren't looking for black market goodies; the river police were looking for him. He didn't hesitate. Taking one of the packages, he slung it with all his strength at the slatternly woman. She yelled with surprise. But she recovered swiftly. He saw her grab the precious tobacco, worth a small fortune in the black market district around Hamburg's Dammtor Station, at the same moment that the big policeman yelled a command. It was just the distraction he needed.

In a racing dive like the one that had habitually won him the 100-yard swimming race at Dartmouth, he was over the side and racing all out for the opposite bank, blind to everything but the overwhelming knowledge that he was fighting for his very life.

The towpath and bank loomed up in front of him: a stretch of frozen white Elbe sand, a shabby church and a clutter of medieval

48

half-timbered houses with fishing nets hanging outside to be repaired or dried.

'Halt,' a harsh angry voice commanded behind him. 'Halt oder ich schiesse, Mensch.'

Savage, going all out, ignored the command. Behind him the engines of the police launch burst into noisy life. The slovenly woman yelled something, but Savage couldn't make it out. He thought afterwards that she had shouted. 'Give 'em one in the kisser, brave boy ... Fuck 'em.'

The cigarette diversion must have worked, because someone was refusing to hurry to cast off the line attaching the launch to the barge. Savage plunged on desperately.

He slammed into the steep slippery bank. A shot rang out. He ignored it. The slug howled off the cobbles a foot or two away in a shower of furious red sparks. Still he kept going, clambering up the bank for all he was worth.

The cop was rattled. He fired again. This time he was even wider. Below the launch, freed at last though a little alarmed and out of control, Savage had managed to knock the river policeman off his aim yet even more. Savage didn't give him time to recover. He sprang on to the towpath and started running, scattering river water everywhere. A woman, pushing a pram like a wickerwork basket on wheels, came towards him. She screamed. Savage didn't hesitate. He punched her brutally. She fell backwards, revealing her naked thighs and patched bloomers. The basket pram wobbled and went slowly over the side towards the river, the hidden baby inside screaming its head off furiously. Savage didn't even hear.

Suddenly he skidded to a halt. A man was standing in the field to his right. He was wearing a green Loden coat and a hat with a feather sticking out of it. He looked like some small-time farmer enjoying a day off, decked out in his rustic finery – and he was carrying a shotgun crooked over his right shoulder!

For one long instant the two men confronted each other. Savage watched the kaleidoscope of emotions – shock, fear, determination, anger – flash across the German's honest, ruddy face. The farmer pulled the shotgun off his shoulder. He fired. One ... two ... both barrels.

The twin muzzles erupted in blasts of scarlet flame. Vicious little lead pellets whizzed everywhere. Savage yelped with pain. He had been hit everywhere. He did the only thing available to him. He dived back into the icy water. Next moment he was swimming for his life while the farmer, trying frantically to reload his shotgun before Savage got away, was yelling, 'Over here … the shit's here…'

By now Savage was beyond caring. He was determined never to go into the bag again. He'd rather die. He felt himself possessed of that old red blinding rage, which had been his downfall in the past. All of a sudden, though, he spotted a way out. A kind of culvert, a dark stone chamber on the side of the bank. The flags worn by the river and time, covered with slippery dark-green moss. Just as a burst of machine gun fire scythed the surface of the water, Savage dived. Above him the slugs whipped the river into an angry, wide whirlpool. He went down further. His flailing hands hit and caught on to a big square-shaped stone. He'd found the entrance to the chamber. Next moment, he was clambering inside and, slipping and slithering, he was moving deeper and deeper into the darkness, heavy with the stench of centuries.

Flame erupted behind him like a blossoming scarlet bloom. The noise of the chattering machine pistol blasting away was earsplitting. Slugs howled off the ancient flags everywhere. Savage, gasping frantically, breath croaking through leathern lungs like that of an ancient asthmatic, slipped round the bend in the tunnel just in time.

'I can hear him,' someone cried excitedly.

'Put a sock in it, arse-with-ears,' another

voice shouted angrily. 'We'll never hear the shit if you kick up that racket.'

Savage didn't hear. With the last of his ebbing strength, he ran on blindly. Now he was solely intent in putting as much space as possible between himself and his pursuers. On and on he blundered, gasping for breath. All around him in the stinking half-darkness, there was a confusion of pipes and tubes. All were covered with an ugly white dripping fungus. The slime of generations seemed to be covering them.

Behind him, magnified tenfold by the hollow tunnel, he could hear the clatter of heavy boots. They were still after him. Desperately he twisted and turned. In and out of high-roofed chambers, the slime-green walls rushing by in a crazed phantasmagoria.

He felt like screaming. Would they never give up? Madly he tried to keep control of himself. But he was weakening fast. He felt hot tears of self-pity fill his eyes.

Abruptly his feet went from beneath him. There was no saving himself. He was in space without a hold. Screaming, now in absolute panic, he found himself falling ... falling ... falling.

With a hellish splash he hit the pit filled with water far below. He went under, desperately fighting for breath. For a moment he panicked, terrified he was going to drown, nostrils filled with the stench of long-stagnant water. But only for a moment. He broke surface, splashing frantically, to realise that he had fallen into some kind of long-abandoned drainage ditch.

With an effort of sheer naked willpower, he calmed himself. He floundered on the surface, taking stock of his circumstances. He struck out for the side. It seemed miles away. His arms sought the reassurance of a solid object. Just when he thought he was going to go under once more, his nails rasped against rough, worked stone. It was the side. With the last of his strength he held on. In that same moment as he took hold, the crunch of heavy nailed boots came level with him, high above his dripping head.

He took a deep breath. He ducked his head beneath the green scum, which parted and then closed above him almost instantly. The sound of the boots stopped. There was a faint mumble of distorted voices. A beam from a torch flashed down the pit. It swept across the surface of the green scum. Beneath it Savage could see the faint glow. He held his breath, ears pounding. With one hand he held on to the side of the pit, body motionless. The beam seemed to hover above him for an age. He knew his breath wouldn't hold out much longer. His lungs were bursting. Now red and silver stars were beginning to explode inside his head. He screamed out within himself for the beam to move on. When it seemed he couldn't last any longer, it did. The boots vanished.

He forced himself to count to five. Next moment he broke the surface with a great splash, gasping for air, breathing in the noxious foul-smelling substance in great grateful gulps. But there was triumph on his soaked, emaciated face. For the time being, he had thrown off his pursuers once again. The Hun bastards still hadn't got him...

A hundred miles away, in the prison block at Hamburg's Altona Jail, Müller watched with seeming boredom the interrogation of the recaptured escaper from the Wesertimke Camp. He was a mere boy, fair-haired and blue-eyed – a perfect Nordic type, Müller couldn't help thinking – who didn't look old enough to have been shot down as a bomber pilot and taken prisoner. Now the boy was at the end of his tether. His right eye was blackened and through his torn shirt, Müller could see the bruised darkened flesh where he had been routinely roughed up by his captors. For the boy, it must have come as a shock to have been beaten up like that, but the average continental, Müller knew, expected the punishment for having caused the Secret Police trouble; it was standard operating procedure.

Müller continued to smoke moodily, while the interrogators' questions were translated into English for the benefit of the prisoner, who didn't speak much German. In the corner, the female secretary with the good legs typed his answers. It was all a great bore. Besides, he had realised within five minutes that the Tommy kid would be of no use for his purpose. First of all, he wasn't even British Navy. Still, dutiful cop, as he was, the head of the Gestapo listened.

At the POW camp, they had planned the great escape for months. The original intention, according to the prisoner, had been to send out over a hundred men. In the end the planners had reduced the number of escapers to fifty. To simplify papers and other items of escape, the Tommy planners had decided on three escape routes and destinations: the nearest was over the border into occupied Holland where the escaper would make contact with 'the Dutch Resistance'.

Müller had allowed himself a hollow, cynical laugh at that, as the crestfallen boy's answer had been translated. Most of the Dutch did as they were told, glad of full employment and full bellies now ensured by the German war industries working all out in their 'conquered' homeland. Indeed so many Dutch were now so taken by their supposed 'occupiers' that they had volunteered to form a whole SS division. As for the 'resistance', it was made up of work-shy individuals, petty crooks and adventurers on the make.

Then there was the escape route south and the Tommies' conviction that they would be received with open arms once they had crossed from the Reich into the neutral 'Home of the Cuckoo Clock'. Again, they were mistaken. For the Swiss, venal as they were, would sell their own grandmother for money. They had their 'little francs', as they called their currency, for hearts. Besides the Swiss sold over sixty per cent of their exports to the Reich and were major supporters of Hitler's war industry. They were not going to risk such financial gains for the sake of a couple of escaped Tommy POWs who were still wet behind the ears in that naive English manner of theirs.

Müller took out his cheap working man's cigar, one of the makes that he favoured, and looked at the spittle-damp end, as if he could see something important there. No, he concluded, it would be the naval types he wanted: those who were heading for Lubeck and Wismar and the other small Baltic ports that traded with neutral Sweden. There he'd find the kind of Englishman he needed to carry out the plan he had begun to formulate in his devious peasant mind ever since that old fart, Raeder, had told him about the break-out and attack of Germany's surface fleet. This pathetic fly boy was useless as far as he was concerned.

Outside, the music in the *Reeperbahn* had commenced. Hamburg's pleasure area, home of pimps, pros and prosperous black marketeers, was frowned upon in the great port's more respectable quarters. How could such a disgraceful place be allowed when Germany's sons were dying in their hundreds at the front? This is what the good honest National Socialist citizens snorted. But Naval High Command knew that such a place had to exist for the pleasures of its sailors on leave. They were risking their lives, too, daily, fighting the Tommies – and there were no brothels on board ship. Hence the *Reeperbahn*, a couple of kilometres of sordid, cheap, quick thrills for sailors with too much pay in their wallets and easily excitable tools in their trousers!

Slowly the noise started to rise. It came at a good time, Müller told himself, swinging his legs off the table of the little makeshift interrogation room. It'd drown any noise the boy made when he was liquidated. He squashed out his cigar in the over-flowing ashtray and nodded to the *Scharführer*, a brutal-faced thug, who was doing the actual interrogation. 'Get rid of the interpreter,' he said softly.

The secretary paused, hands in the air, and looked at him and then back at the boy. Suddenly Müller thought she had a soft look on her middle-aged mug. Typical, he told himself. Women were no good for this kind of job.

The boy looked puzzled. He had expected the relentless interrogation from the ugly-faced thug to continue. Why had it stopped so abruptly? Surely they wanted to get more out of him. They knew he hadn't finished 'singing like a yellow canary', as the interpreter had translated the SS man's contemptuous phrase.

Müller didn't enlighten the kid. He couldn't speak English anyway. Still he felt sorry for the young Tommy. It was not that he was a soft touch. Not as the head of the Gestapo. It was simply because the kid was like so many he had watched being questioned in his twenty-odd years of police service. They never woke up to the fact that this was the end of the road; they had said their last words, smoked their last 'lung torpedo', taken their last few breaths. There was nothing more. They were dead men already. That was the sad bit. Their life had come to an end and they didn't even know it.

He waited till the interpreter and the

secretary, with the nice legs, filed by him and then he nodded to the *Scharführer*, who would carry out the execution. Why bother with a trial? It would be a waste of money. The outcome would be the same. The *Scharführer* nodded back his understanding, while the kid watched the silent interchange in bewilderment.

Müller picked up his cap with its gleaming skull-and-crossbones silver badge. He passed out into the busy street, barely acknowledging the salutes of the two fat, middle-aged policemen standing there in their black leather helmets. Things were livening up in the crowded street. There were sailors and whores everywhere, grinning professionally, haggling in street corners, dragging off already drunken young gobs to their rooms to dance a quick 'mattress polka' at ten marks a go. 'Nothing too good for our boys in the service,' they chortled, as they lifted their skirts to show their fat dimpled naked arses.

But Gestapo Müller saw hardly anything of this. His mind and mind's eye were elsewhere. He knew what he had to do. Moscow had been overjoyed, according to his control, when he had passed on to Beria – the head of the dreaded Russian secret police – the information he had received from Grand Admiral Raeder. But how was he going to

59

carry out the plan he and his control had formulated without risking his own neck? It had to be foolproof. Russia hadn't won the war by a long chalk. Indeed she hadn't really entered it. At the moment Hitler and his Third Reich dominated most of Europe. For the time being he had to be careful, exceedingly careful. If anything went wrong, even the long arm of the NKVD wouldn't be able to save him.

There was a pause in the roll and drum-beat of the great Dutch organ outside the Moulin Rouge, a strange sudden – somehow awesome – silence, broken only by the snap of a single shot like that of a dry twig cracking underfoot in a summer forest. Müller knew instinctively what it was: the *Scharführer* blowing the back of the Tommy kid's head off in the prison courtyard.

An instant later the merry clatter of the Dutch organ started up again and Müller continued walking – even the drunks getting out of his way, for the little man with the enormous, shaven head and the dark sinister eyes had Gestapo written all over him. And no one, drunk or otherwise, wanted to fall foul of the Secret State Police.

Four

Every pace was sheer agony. The sudden snow came down in blinding white sheets. Desperately, he cleared the wet flakes from his face and eyes time and time again. But the wind continued to rage. Ever anew it whipped the snow against his frozen, wolfish features. Shivering almost uncontrollably, Savage carried on. Now it was only by sheer effort and determination that he was able to place one foot in front of the other in the ankle-deep snow.

At first he had been glad of the unseasonable snowstorm. He guessed it would throw the police off his tracks ever since he had left the River Elbe and began heading north-east towards Lubeck. But now the constant snow, beating down in silent fury as if some god up on high was determined to bury him beneath it, had turned into a nightmare. More than once he had been tempted to simply throw himself down in its soft whiteness and sleep ... perhaps for ever.

But he had always caught himself just in

61

time. Through gritted teeth he had snarled, 'No, you Hun bastards ... you won't get me ... I won't die ... Do you hear me? I *won't!*' The words were torn from his mouth by the wind, but the challenge remained. He was going to keep on. *He had to.* And Savage did. He slogged across the seemingly endless North German plain, fighting the merciless snow-heavy wind, a pathetic little creature lost in that howling wilderness.

At two o'clock that afternoon, he knew he couldn't go on. With the sky as black as night and the snow still falling in solid sheets, he took shelter in a small grove of firs that made up the boundary of some side road. Here he tried to take stock of his position.

His camp-made compass – a razorblade magnetised in a light socket and a piece of stiff cardboard from one of the Swiss Red Cross parcels, paid for by the British tax-payer – functioned perfectly. He was still well on course on the left bank of the Elbe, heading for the two bridges crossing the river eastwards at Lauenburg. Here it would be his intention to cross the river by the rail-way bridge, which he guessed wouldn't be guarded, and head north-east for the Baltic coast, some fifty or so kilometres away.

It was then that he looked down at his 'civvies': a dyed black battledress suit, which had been stained with printer's ink. Now the ink had run and was patchy from the effects of the sewage in the conduit. In this outfit, as it was now, he knew he'd stand out like a sore thumb once he got among the Germans again. And he knew, too, that sooner or later he'd have to mingle with them when he reached the Baltic searching for a Swedish ship. Besides the whole damn outfit stank to high heavens. 'No, old man,' he said softly to himself in the manner of lonely – or mad – people who speak to themselves a lot, 'you've got to get yerself some other clobber ... and you've got to get out of this blasted freezing snow before your goolies drop off.'

That particularly terrible thought gave him a new burst of energy. If he moved closer to the river somewhere to his right, he'd be bound to find inhabited places; there were always houses close to a river, especially one which was a major trade route as the Elbe was. There, there would be clothes. But would he be able to buy them with the marks stuffed into his breast pocket, the result of months spent bribing guards by means of his cigarette ration? He doubted it. He had an uneasy feeling that the Huns had clothing coupons just as the folk back home did. Money wouldn't be very useful then. He bit his cracked chapped lip and winced at the sudden pain. There was only one other alternative. His hand slid into his trouser pocket and felt the cold lethal hardness of the jack-knife that rested there. If there was no other way, well...

An hour later, the fugitive spotted the yellow gleam of a petroleum lamp shining through the scraggy, snow-heavy firs to his right. He paused wearily. He wiped the wet snowflakes from his face to get a better view.

It was a typical red brick-and-wattle construction of the area. Low and long, it had yellow dried tobacco leaves drying under its eaves and, from the building towards the end of the dwelling area there, with steam rising from the tiny open window slats, came the warm animal smell of cows. It was obviously a small, one-family farm with both the humans and the animals living under the same roof.

The thought of warmth and hot food made Savage shiver with anticipation. All the same he forced himself to watch the lonely little farm for a solid half-hour while the snow fell softly and, sadly, muting the sound of the cows. It was occupied, he could see that. There was thick blue wood smoke coming from the main chimney and there were tracks, already disappearing quickly in the snow, around the main door. But how many people were there in the place? He couldn't even guess. All he could surmise was that such a small farm wouldn't be able to support more than a farmer and his wife, plus one of the Polish or French prisoners-of-war being hired out by the local *Kreisleiter* as a labourer.

In the end, after he had seen nothing move for nearly three-quarters of an hour, with his body turning to ice as he crouched there, he decided it was now or never. Soon it would be dark and he didn't want to be surprised in the act by some latecomer arriving at the house after work or such like. It was time to go,

Cautiously, open jack-knife clutched to his right hip, he moved through the snow, grateful that it muffled any sound he might make as he passed through the open gate and advanced upon the old farm. Foot by foot he crept ever closer. There was no sound save the hiss of the snowstorm and the wind in the skeletal trees. Inside the house nothing stirred. No one had even moved to put up the blackout, though perhaps in this remote area, they didn't worry about such things.

Suddenly there was a low growl, accompanied by the rattle of a chain to his right. 'A bloody dog,' he cursed.

Behind the barn a dog of some kind was presumably tied up and, despite the snowstorm, it had obviously scented him. In half a minute it would begin barking and sounding the alarm. There was no time for further

65

caution. He had to act *now*!

Throwing all caution to the wind, panting hard, as if he were running a great race, he flung open the door, knife held aloft, ready to plunge it into the body of anyone who attempted to oppose him.

Sitting next to the great tiled oven which reached to the ceiling, the old crone dropped her knitting in panic. Her bent hand flew to her scraggy, veined throat.

Savage was taking no chances. Even as her yellowed teeth bulged from her trembling lips in abject fear, he advanced upon her. Meaningless words tumbled from her quavering mouth.

'Listen,' he cried in his best German. 'You scream ... I kill ... *Verstanden*?' He slashed the air viciously with his knife to make his meaning clear. The saliva of fear started to trickle in streams from her wrinkled hairy chin. '*Verstanden*?' he rasped again.

The old woman didn't trust herself to speak. She nodded her head rapidly. Savage relaxed and lowered the knife.

'Other men ... women here?' he queried.

The old crone pulled herself together. She understood that the stranger wasn't going to slit her skinny throat after all. She shook her head and managed to croak, '*Nee*.'

Savage gave her a fake smile and, very slowly and deliberately, while she watched, hypnotised, he closed the jack-knife and carefully put it in his pocket. Now he placed both hands deliberately on the warm tiles of the *Kachelofen*. It was another gesture to show the crone that he intended her no harm, if she behaved herself. '*Hunger*,' he said loudly, as if he were talking to an idiot ... '*Essen ... bitte...*'

She understood. She rose with an audible creak of ancient bones. Still terrified, she smoothed her way past this soaked, un-shaven intruder and fled into the kitchen. Moments later he watched through the open door as she held a great round loaf of dark bread – 'a wheel', the Huns called it – to her weak breast and sliced off the chunks, while in front of her on the wooden stove, the salt bacon lumps sizzled nicely.

For the first time since he had escaped from the camp, Lieutenant-Commander Savage smiled. 'Thank God for old Adolf,' he muttered to himself, 'he certainly taught the female of the species where her place is – in the kitchen.'

So it was that for a while Savage, at peace at last, lounged outside the open kitchen door, watching the old crone and sniffing the delightful smells coming from the old iron, wood-burning stove with mouthwatering anticipation.

But only for so long...

Despite the howl of the wind, Savage heard the steps crunching slowly over the frozen snow of the little path that led up to the door. There was someone coming. Suddenly he was one hundred per cent alert, the adrenalin surging through his tired body. He flashed a look at the woman. She had heard nothing. She was devoting herself whole-heartedly to the task of frying his chunks of *Speck* and the *Bratkartoffeln* which she had mixed with the pieces of salt bacon. Obviously she wasn't expecting anyone at this time. Otherwise her brain, old as it was, would have been prepared for someone coming and she would have recognised the sound already. So who was it?

Savage didn't know. All he knew was that the approaching footsteps spelled danger.

He grabbed for his knife, thought better of it and, glancing around wildly, spotted one of those great paddles German housewives used to beat their carpets. That would do. One blow from that and there would be no dangerous grappling with whomever was now approaching the door. He'd be out like a light with a bit of luck. Then when he had dealt with the unknown visitor, he could decide what to do next. Taking a deep breath, he grasped the wooden paddle more firmly.

The footsteps halted. He heard the scraping, once, twice. The visitor was clearing the snow away from his feet on the old-fashioned scraper. Savage held his breath. The door was beginning to open. '*Oma*,' a cheerful, rather light voice called, '*Ich bin...*'

Savage raised the beater. His hand felt wet with sweat.

'Granny,' the voice called again. In the kitchen the old woman turned, a sudden beam on her wrinkled old face. '*Ach, du bist*—'

Savage caught a glimpse of a slim body muffled in an old Polish Army greatcoat and surmounted by a pretty glowing face. But even before the old crone could complete her welcome, the beater came slamming down and the woman was reeling against the wall, face suddenly pale with shock, her silk blonde hair abruptly turning red with blood...

Five

'*Here the shitehawks come agen,*' the *Obermaat* yelled above the sudden roar of massed plane engines. '*Off port bow ... green five-O ... Lead 'em into it, yer bunch of frigging candy asses ... Look lively now!*'

Standing on the deck next to Rear Admiral Doenitz, head of the submarine service, Grand Admiral Raeder shook his head, as if he couldn't believe his own ears. 'How coarse these new sailors have become, Doenitz,' he said severely. 'In my days, any petty officer using that kind of language would be behind Swedish curtains,' he meant the bars of a jail, 'very quickly indeed.' He shook his greying head once again.

'*Jawohl, Herr Grossadmiral,*' Doenitz answered dutifully, though in fact, he had nothing but contempt for his superior and his old-fashioned attitude. He didn't give a damn how much his U-boat boys cursed, damned and fornicated, as long as they continued sending plenty of Tommy ships to the bottom of the sea.

70

The Tommy bombers were coming in at the usual height, which the flak concentrated upon without much difficulty. As Doenitz told himself, the English were methodical, pedantic creatures; they always stuck to the same sort of tactics. Now the ship's anti-aircraft guns were rounding away with routine precision throwing up a lethal chain-mesh of shot and shell in front of the first V of Wellington bombers. Still, as routine as they were, the Tommy pilots were brave fools; they kept on coming.

Down below the *Obermaat* in charge of the quadruple twenty millimetre flak cannons – blasting away at a tremendous rate so that the tracer shells seemed to be shooting upwards in a solid wall of white fury – was yelling above the hellish racket, 'Hit the buggers, or by the Great Whore of Buxtehudem where the dogs piss through their ribs, I'll take the vaseline to your pansy asses this very night. If it's the last frigging thing I do, I swear I will!'

Doenitz's cold, calculating face cracked into a grin again. That particular *Obermaat* would be losing his 'stars' in zero, comma, nothing, if he kept swearing like that in front of Grand Admiral Raeder. The old naval chief was like some virginal well-born old maid. Next moment the grin disappeared from Doenitz's face almost as soon as it had appeared.

The Tommies were trying a new tactic. Under the cover of the approaching V of Wellington bombers, on which the ship's anti-aircraft artillery was concentrating all its fire, three old-fashioned biplanes had appeared from the smoke of battle. They were coming in at seatop level. Their propellors lashed the sea below into a white fury, as they swerved from side to side, laden down as they were with a great two-ton torpedo fixed beneath their undercarriage.

'Swordfish!' Raeder breathed. 'I thought the English Navy had withdrawn them from service because last year's fiasco up north.' He meant the battle for Norway.

'Doesn't look like it, sir,' Doenitz said, face set and sombre now. Although his love affair with his U-boats was almost all-embracing, he *was* a member of the German Navy; and he knew these obsolete British planes could inflict tremendous damage on even these most modern of German ships, especially if they got lucky with their damned all-powerful 'tin fish'.

Raeder knew it, too. He turned and, with surprising energy for such an old pedantic officer, he yelled to his orderly, 'Lieutenant, at the double. Get the gunner officer. Switch flak on to those damned flying canvas bags.'

'Sir.' The young elegant officer immediately flew across the ship's deck, littered with battle debris, towards the ladder that led up to the gunnery officer's control room, as if the Devil himself were at his heels. To starboard the old-fashioned British planes, wave-hopping now, came on with grim determination...

'Well,' Commander Jensen asked, as 'Pox' waddled into the wardroom, totally unconcerned by the English attack, 'how's Old Wheels' – he meant Raeder – 'getting on? After all, he's not used to having all this Tommy shit flung at him.'

'Pox', otherwise Surgeon-Lieutenant von Mauz, one of the great ship's doctors, said, 'Shitty.' He sat down abruptly and helped himself to one of the bottles of schnapps on the silver tray right beneath the forbidding gaze of the Führer, who, as everyone knew, hated alcohol. He pulled put the cork with his excellent teeth and poured himself a stiff peg. '*Prost*,' he said to himself, and downed the fiery liquid in one go. He gasped and said, 'That hit the frigging spot.'

Commander Jensen affected concern and disapproval. 'I say, Doctor,' he intoned. 'It's not yet zero ten hundred hours. Bit early for the old fire-water, isn't it?'

'My guts can't tell the time,' the bespectacled Pox replied sourly.

Jensen smiled sympathetically. He could

understand how the MO felt. He was responsible for the VD rate on board the ship. It was an unenviable position. There were two certainties in the life of the average sailor in the German Navy: he was going to get drunk and he was going to get a dose. It was the nature of the beast and all the threats and punishments in this world couldn't stop either eventuality. 'Siff rate gone up again?' he enquired politely. He took a sip of his coffee.

Despite the Führer's forbidding gaze, Pox helped himself to another stiff drink. 'No, it's that arse-with-ears Doenitz.'

'Tut, tut,' Jensen admonished him. 'Not our beloved U-boat Führer.'

'Yes, he's talking to Old Wheels ten to the dozen. They don't even seem to notice the Tommies dropping square eggs on their heads.'

'So?'

'So,' Pox answered hotly, 'he's trying to put one over on Old Wheels. You know, Doenitz and those U-boats of his. He thinks that the sun shines out of the arse of his submariners. It's the only war he knows and if we get shafted in his attempts to give them the premier place in the sea war, then it's hard shit for us.'

'My dear Pox,' Commander Jensen said with apparent ease, but all the same his handsome face looked worried, 'your years of looking at the diseased sexual organs of generations of naughty sailors have coarsened you, old chap. But be that as it may, what can we do about it—'

But before the MO could answer that particular question, a burning biplane came flashing by the nearest porthole, trailing a scarlet, searing flame behind it. An instant later the whole great ship rocked like a child's toy ship on a lake, as it exploded, torpedo and all, sending the two officers sliding the length of the wardroom, accompanied by breaking bottles and glasses. Up above Grand Admiral Raeder desperately clung on to the rail, as the ship heaved and wallowed, debris flying everywhere, with the severed Tommy pilot's head racing across the sky in front of him, complete with leather helmet and severed wireless leads.

Next to Raeder the much younger and more agile Doenitz recovered swiftly, saying a little breathlessly, 'I think we've cured that particular Tommy flyboy's headache for him – *permanently*.'

Raeder watched as the head struck the water, bounced a couple of times and then vanished. He said severely, 'He was some mother's son, I shouldn't doubt.'

'Old fart,' an angry voice at the back of Doenitz's shaven head rasped in sudden anger, 'why does he frigging well moralise to me?' He remembered the Führer's words to him the last time he had attended one of his conferences at his mountain fastness in the remote Bavarian Alps. 'Doenitz,' the leader had intoned solemnly, 'I wish all my soldiers were like your "Blue Boys" ' – he had meant Doenitz's submariners – 'as tough as Krupp steel, as fast as greyhounds and hard as leather. This nation will go under unless it is more ruthless, purposeful and murderous than its opponents.' And then he had added something *sotto voce* so that the other brass present couldn't hear, 'My eye, Doenitz, rests very favourably on you and your command – it may well be that I shall call upon you sooner than you think.'

Doenitz had long learned to distrust the veiled promises of great men, but he had thought that the Führer had been making him an offer, that if Raeder failed with his surface ships, he would take over with his 'Blue Boys' and start a campaign of unrestricted warfare, which he had long advocated and which would finally bring the damned buck-teethed English down to their knees where they had long damned well belonged.

Another obsolete British torpedo bomber had come winging in through the drifting anti-aircraft smoke, specked with cherry-red spurts of exploding shells. It, too, was flying at wave-level, dragging its prop wash behind it. Doenitz flung up his binoculars, the look of the hunter suddenly on his lean hard face. He could see the face of the pilot and then that of the observer slide noiselessly into the gleaming calibrated rings of the glass. They were set and determined: the look of two men doomed to a sudden death.

Doenitz felt no pity. Indeed he was animated by the opposite: a feeling burning rage. How dare the Tommies attack Germany's ships like this at their home anchorage? They deserved to die – and soon.

They did. The gunners concentrated all their fire on the lone, slow plane. They knew if that enormous torpedo hit them, they were done for. Now they poured a murderous hail of hot steel on the plane, as it came in on its final ride of death. At that range, they simply could not miss.

Great chunks of metal started to fly from the Swordfish's fuselage. The rigging went. The wings flapping almost out of control. Desperately, his face contorted under the leather helmet, the young pilot fought to keep the stricken plane from plunging into the sea. 'What a brave young fool,' Raeder said, as if to himself, as he adjusted the setting of his glasses. 'Why doesn't he jump for it, while he still has time?'

Doenitz's face flushed with anger. God, Raeder was already in his dotage. When did you win a war by having pity on your enemies? *Hate* – that was the name of the game. You had to hate your enemy with every damned fibre of your body. It was the only way.

Now the plane was beginning to burn. Greedy little blue flames were beginning to lick up about the fuselage. Smoke, white and thick, was already pouring from the engine. It was only a matter of moments. Nothing could save the Tommy plane. But would the pilot be able to loose his torpedo before his Swordfish went totally out of control and dropped into the sea? Doenitz felt himself start to sweat heavily. His hands gripping the binoculars abruptly turned into white-knuckled claws. He was suddenly panting as if he were running a great race. He gasped. He's doing it!

The pilot was. In his dying moments, he had thrown all concern about the safety of himself and his observer to the winds. Slowly he was hand-cranking the torpedo, jammed a little between the wheels of the shattered undercarriage, down and down so that he was then in a position to fire it – and at that range, he couldn't possibly miss.

But now his luck had run out. Just as he had cleared the wheels with his torpedo, the

Obermaat with the 'loose, filthy tongue', as Raeder had snapped, pulled off a feat which would earn him the Iron Cross, First Class, from the Führer himself, though he would never live to receive it personally from that quarter. Under his direction, a massive burst of nearly 1,000 twenty millimetre cannon shells from the quadruple flak gun slammed straight into the stricken plane. It disappeared in an instant. One minute it was there; the next it wasn't. All that remained of it was the patter of shattered metal striking the surface of the sea for a few moments like a heavy tropical downpour. And then all was silent...

Five minutes later it was all over. The ship's sirens were sounding the all-clear. Fire control parties in their heavy fire-proof suits looking like creatures from an alien planet rushed back and forth; while on the quays the ambulance from Wilhelmshaven's naval hospital rushed to the scene of the bombing, sirens shrieking their urgent warning.

Slowly, thoughtfully, automatically dodging the battle debris which now littered the once spotless deck of the great ship, the two admirals walked back to their quarters, deep frowns on both their faces. Jensen, watching them from the open door of the wardroom, said to 'Pox', 'They look like some of your patients, who have just been told they've got a full house, gon and siff.'

Pox ignored the dig. Instead he said, 'Look at Doenitz. The cunning bugger's up to something – you can see that on his shitting Polack face.'

Jensen eyed the U-boat commander with his high Slavic cheekbones and sharp features, telling himself Doenitz's mouth always seemed to be worked by a tight steel spring. Yes, he concluded that the younger Admiral did have a Polish look about him. 'Wonder what they're talking about, Pox?' he asked.

'Nothing good for Old Wheels, you can bet your bottom dollar on that,' the little MO replied. 'Doenitz is up to his old tricks. Sooner or later he's gonna find the right tack and then Old Wheels will be out on his neck and we big ship folk will be out there with him.' He shivered dramatically. 'Fancy being a medic in one of Doenitz's subs.'

Like so many other big ship sailors, Jensen was terrified at the thought of being posted to Doenitz's underwater tin cans. 'We've got to do something about it,' he said after a few moments of watching the two admirals disappear towards their own state rooms.

'What?'

'Well, like trying to stop Doenitz talking Old Wheels into doing something which will spell the end – or mothballing the surface fleet.'

'What, for instance?' Pox asked bluntly,

suddenly remembering that in an hour's time he had to administer what the sailors called the 'umbrella' to half a dozen unfortunates.

'How do I know?' Jensen blurted out in sudden worriedy irritation. 'Am I Jesus? Do I walk on water? All I know is that Doenitz is up to no shitting good.'

And Commander Karl Jensen was right. Doenitz had plans. And they didn't bode well for Grand Admiral Raeder and his surface ships.

Six

Gestapo Müller was angry. Not in that flushed, loud-mouthed excitable manner he used both to frighten and impress prisoners. Now his anger was a low-key burn that no one else but he might have noticed. But this kind of anger in a man of his nature, and with the vast power he commanded, was of a much more deadly kind. It was that type of rage that, in the past, had impelled him to order the destruction of whole villages and the systematic slaughter of their helpless populations. And, as usual with Gestapo Müller, this slow burning rage had been occasioned by very small and relatively unimportant matters.

Two hours before he had felt the need for sexual relief. It was a problem of no great moment. But in his peasant fashion, he felt that one satiation of this physical need would ensure great mental ability. So it was that he turned to the senior officers' brothel located in a fine old turn-of-the-century house overlooking the harbour.

It had been a bad mistake. Right from the start he had realised that he had been unwelcome there, although he was prepared to pay for the services offered instead of trying to avoid payment like most Gestapo officers did, who traded on their fearsome reputation to get what they wanted.

The other officers, drinking and smoking their cigars, occasionally glancing at the racked newspapers while they waited their turn to be called upstairs, ignored him and even the Madam, big bosomy and blousy treated him like some village yokel who had wandered into her 'establishment' by mistake.

The whore she had allotted him – 'very much your type, *Standartenführer*,' she had assured him, 'a good hard-working girl, ready to put her heart into it' – had turned out to be disappointing.

She had been fat, flabby with pendulous breasts, the nipples painted bright red and hanging down to her belly folds of lard. Even as she prepared to slump into the untidy stained bed with him, she had continued eating her chocolates, as if her very life depended upon it, licking her nicotine-stained fingers after every supposedly delicate bite. As Müller had loosened his trousers belt, he had told himself grimly, 'This is going to be like climbing shitting Mount Everest without the shitting oxygen.' And his description of the act hadn't proved far wrong.

In the end, the whore had promised a 'free go' next time 'when you're in better mood, *Standartenführer*' but had obstinately refused to return to him even part of the agreed-upon price. The Gestapo had obviously cut no ice with her. She had called after him as he had slunk somewhat shamefacedly down the stairs, avoiding the looks of the place's other clients, 'You can't expect a working girl to do the impossible, after all, *Standartenführer*,' and he could see from the expression on the others' faces that they had supposed he had demanded some impossible perversion from the whore. Even as he had hurried to his waiting staff car, his ears were burning as he imagined what they were already relating *sotto voce* to their fellows.

But the unfortunate incident with the local whore paled in Müller's mind in comparison with the other item which occasioned his rage this dark winter's afternoon. It was really a failing on his own part and Gestapo Müller, who had been a professional cop since he was nineteen, hated to slip up on the job.

He knew that he had slipped up badly in the matter of the escaped POWs, when Eichmann, of all people, telephoned him from the Gestapo HQ in Prinz Albrecht Strasse,

Berlin, to point out that the Führer had called personally. Eichmann, the only senior officer present, had taken the phone call and had been on the receiving end of the leader's wrath when the latter had discovered that there were still so many escapers at liberty.

According to Eichmann, who Müller thought was a typical Austrian lightweight with a head full of crazy ideas like his countryman, Hitler, the Führer had snorted, 'Do you expect me to tell you damned policemen your own job? Haven't I got enough problems on my hands running a war, Eichmann?'

Eichmann, petrified at speaking to the Führer personally – Müller had guessed he'd probably been standing to attention as he had held the phone – had mumbled some-thing and had waited apprehensively.

He had related Hitler's words to his boss, Müller. 'The Führer said, "The matter is quite simple. It only needs a bit of common sense to round these Tommy criminals up within twenty-four hours at the most".'

Müller had been inclined to interrupt his subordinate, but then he thought better of it – could he trust Eichmann? – and had held his peace.

'The Führer said, "It's a matter of organ-ising the checks and controls on specific points where one could expect the escapers to appear as they make their way to their various objectives. Seal off the area purposefully and logically, instead of wasting men and time in mass searches..." ' Eichmann had continued relating the leader's words, ending with that undeniable threat that the Austrian blowhard, Hitler, always used when thwarted, 'If Müller can't do it, then he'd better let someone else take his place who can.' And with that he had slammed down the phone in one of those blind rages of his, leaving Eichmann trembling with fear and 'heiling' a dead phone for all he was worth.

Still, an angry Müller told himself as he stared out of the big picture window, the Führer was right for a change – he had never paid even lip-service to Hitler's supposed infallibity. There had to be a simple way of ensuring that his unsuspecting Tommy escapers walked right into the net he was preparing for them – and quickly at that.

He turned from the window and strode over to the map of the Baltic area which covered the entire wall behind him. Right from the first instant he could see that anyone moving eastwards from the POW camp at Wesertimke and heading for the Baltic ports and the ships which linked them with neutral Sweden was faced with a major barrier – the natural one of the River Elbe.

Müller frowned and peered a little short-sightedly at the map, trying to make out the bridges which spanned the great waterway in the upper part of the Elbe. Naturally Hamburg looked the easiest option. But only at first sight. There, there were several bridges running from west to east. But anyone trying to reach them would be confronted by the task of covering the length of Germany's second greatest city, full of police, informers and soldiers on duty. Hamburg was out.

The Baltic, 1941

Müller posed there thoughtfully. Outside, despite the weather, a group of half-naked recruits to the *Kriegsmarine* were being put through their paces by a typically sadistic instructor. He was making a right sow out of them.

'Up ... up,' he cried and when the recruits were running, he was already bellowing, 'down ... down,' making them slam to the snowy, slushy ground so that their soaked training uniforms became even wetter. Müller knew the drill; he had been through it himself as a young soldier back in the First World War. Soon they'd be unable to get up, lying there in the dirt panting and exhausted. Then the instructor would approach – with majestic slowness – and shove his big boot in the small of their skinny backs and force their faces into the muck.

Müller, who had tortured more people than he cared to remember in the course of his long career with the police, didn't like it – he didn't like it one bit. It was part of a system, that of the 'monocle Fritzes', which he hated and which, in part, had made him take the dangerous course he had now embarked upon.

Abruptly he dismissed the pathetic recruits and their sadistic taskmaster and concentrated on the job at hand. Again he peered short-sightedly at the big map. No, Hamburg was out, he told himself, and the fugitive wouldn't have the resources and energy to try out the minor bridges along the Elbe which ran through Germany till it reached the sea. He'd have to go for the bridges between – say – Magdeburg in the south up to those below Hamburg around Geesthacht and Lauenburg. Here there was not only a road bridge but a railway bridge, carrying the main line from Berlin to Hamburg.

He tugged at the end of his big nose thoughtfully. Apart from the Hamburg bridges, those at Lauenburg were the ones closest to the camp at Wesertimke, from which the damned Tommies had escaped and caused all the panic. Was Geesthacht-Lauenburg, the point where he should concentrate his forces? Thereafter anyone on the run would have half a dozen Baltic ports to choose from and that would make his task very much more difficult. What was he to do?

Outside the instructor had finished with

making sows of the trainees – for this day. He was shouting, 'When we move off, you shitting asparagus Tarzans, I want a song to impress the CO. And none of yer shitting lame-assed singing. I want yer shouting off the words, as if you frigging well belonged to the frigging *Leibstandarte*.' He meant the premier SS regiment, the Adolf Hitler bodyguard regiment. 'Now then a song – One, two, three ... "*Auf der Heide bluht ein Roselein ... und das heisst Erika...*" '

They joined in. Without enthusiasm. Müller watched them go, trailing dripping water behind them, no strength left in their young bodies. Cannon fodder, he told himself, just rotten old cannon fodder, boys doomed to die young before they had even begun to live.

Then he dismissed them, as if they had never even existed, to concentrate on his current tasks. He scribbled out his orders, which were to be sent out immediately to all Gestapo stations along the line of the Elbe up to Hamburg. His local men would, in their turn, alert the uniformed cops, plus the battalions responsible for the country's internal security in that region. By midday, Müller reasoned, as he scribbled furiously in that tiny, almost illegible handwriting of his, the whole area would be standing by at red alert. The Tommies – he wanted to catch them alive – wouldn't stand a chance now.

By eleven that morning, Müller's rage had passed and he was feeling quite pleased with himself. Things were proceeding smoothly and according to plan. By tomorrow evening he'd be returning home to Berlin to his pious Roman Catholic wife and his very *unpious* secretary-mistress. He smiled coldly at the thought. One way or another, it was going to be an enjoyable weekend.

But just as he was about to get carried away by these thoughts, there was an urgent knock at his door and even before he could call '*Herein*', Milz, his personal assistant burst in, face red and excited, eyes bulging from beneath his bottle-lensed nickel glasses. '*Standartenführer ... Standartenführer ...* important news!'

Müller held up his hands for peace, snapping, 'Hold your horses, Milz. Now get your breath back and tell me what's so important.'

The little man gulped and swallowing his own spit, he said, 'Just come in from our man at Raeder's HQ. You know, sir, that big *Oberkommissar* who drinks so much ... Barthels or what—'

'Get on with it, *please*, Milz.'

'*Jawohl, Standartenführer* ... sorry. Well, sir, Barthels has just called from across the bay. The High Sea Fleet is to pull out first tide tomorrow morning. Zero six hundred hours to be exact.'

'What?'

'Thought you'd be surprised, *Standartenführer*. I nearly popped out of my pants, if you'll forgive the phrase, when I heard it.'

'But where ... where is the fleet going?' Müller stuttered.

'Barthels doesn't know exactly, but the buzz at Old Wheels' HQ is that it's bound for further up the Baltic – Danzig to be exact.'

'*Danzig*,' Müller echoed, totally confused now. 'But why Danzig, for God's sake?'

But the pop-eyed little Gestapo man had no answer to that particular, overwhelming question...

Book Two

Enter James Bond

One

Dawn.

Silent and sinister, the British submarine sailed at periscope depth into the shallows. This was the most dangerous part of the whole mission: the penetration of the Baltic.

One arm hanging over the periscope, battered cap stuck at the back of his head, Lieutenant de Vere turned the instrument through its 360 degrees slowly and carefully. Watching him in the fetid, green-glowing area of the control compartment, any uninitiated observer might have thought the submarine's skipper was terribly complacent and nonchalant – in the best British public school fashion. But de Vere was anything but. At the side of his pale face a nerve was ticking electrically, out of control, and his breath was coming in fast, frightened gasps. For he knew better than most – he had carried out this death-defying mission more than once – just how dangerous the situation was. One slip, one wrong move and he and his crew might well be 'sitting on a frigging cloud learning to play a frigging harp, with St Peter leading the frigging orchestra'.

A satisfied de Vere turned the periscope to survey the block ship anchored to their front. In the sun's thin rays of the new day, it was outlined a stark black, rocking slightly as it rode at anchor. It might well have been abandoned, its crew long gone, leaving it to grow ever more rusty. But the young sub-skipper knew that wasn't the case.

Down below, men like themselves would be busy at their instruments, listening and checking, alert for the slightest indication that some unauthorised intruder was attempting to penetrate the Baltic and the anchorage of the German surface fleet beyond. One signal from the rusty old tub, which creaked alarmingly every time it was hit by a wave and the whole of northern Germany – airforce and fleet – would be alerted. Then all hell would be let loose and HMS *Defiant* would be easy meat in these shallow waters. Soon the posh accent of the BBC's radio announcer would be intoning, 'The Admiralty regrets to announce that one of His Majesty's submarines is reported missing, presumed lost at sea...'

Swiftly de Vere dismissed that unpleasant thought and ordered softly, 'Tube ... down ten.'

Carruthers, de Vere's number one, responded immediately. There was a hiss of compressed air and the shining steel periscope slid down until its head and the gleaming circle of calibrated glass protruded just above the dirty brown water of the entrance to the Baltic.

Now, slowly and silently, praying that the head of the periscope was not making too much of a tell-tale white ripple, de Vere steered the submarine slowly by the block ship. Time seemed to move on leaden feet. Over and over again, he cast a glance through the scope at the German guard ship. But nothing moved there, save a thin trickle of smoke now coming from her stack. It indicated that the cook was in his galley preparing the crew's breakfast. That reassured the young officer; it was perfectly normal. 'All shipshape and Bristol fashion?' his number one asked.

De Vere, arms hung over the periscope, nodded, 'Yes. Only I wish they'd put out some buoys to indicate the channel.'

'Mines?' his second-in-command uttered the dread word.

'Yes, mines,' the skipper answered, forcing himself to fight against superstition. He didn't want to join all the other average submariners in their rows to avoid words that could bring upon disaster if spoken aloud. Nor was he going to indulge himself in all the other talismans of the submarine service – teddies, silk stockings, lucky rabbits' feet and all the rest of the junk with which his men hoped to ward off doom. Constant alertness was the only answer.

They ploughed on. Now they were beginning to leave the rusty old tub behind them. To the east, the sky was getting brighter. That was good. He reasoned that decent weather would bring the crab and shrimp fishermen out from Emden and Cuxhaven and the other coastal fishing ports. An unarmed fishing boat on its own, manned by a couple of crew, would be just what he needed.

Again time crept by leadenly. Now that they had left the block ship behind and that there were no other signs of danger in the vicinity, the crew began to relax. Here and there men whistled tonelessly as they carried out their duties. Back in the crews' cramped quarters the smell of bangers tempted the men. Sausages, even navy issue 'pussers', always cheered the boys up, de Vere, still at the periscope, told himself. There might even be a fried egg thrown in. Now *that* would be a real treat!

Suddenly, startlingly, he caught his breath at a noise. It was very faint, but there was no mistaking it. Metal grating against metal. Instantly a cold finger of fear traced its way down the small of de Vere's hunched back. For a moment he thought his imagination was playing tricks upon him. But when that dread sound came again and a look of fear flashed across his number one's ashen face, he knew it wasn't. He reacted immediately. 'Stop engines,' he hissed.

Number one echoed the order urgently.

The engines died. The sub's pace stopped almost immediately. But the terrible sound didn't go away. Now, instead of the grating of metal on metal, there was a soft steel knocking noise on the hull. De Vere knew what it was, but it was for Chalky White to put the name of the sound into words. 'Christ,' he hissed, 'a chained mine!'

The start of fear at the announcement was almost tangible. Instantly all eyes were focused on the young skipper. De Vere was as afraid as the rest, though. There was little even a skipper could do in such a situation.

They had run into a minefield; with mines – rather than floating loose as they might do in an enemy war zone, their acoustics activated and propelling them towards enemy vessels – anchored at regular depths to prevent any intruder penetrating the position. With a loose mine, a cool-headed skipper might stand a chance. But with a tethered mine, the submarine commander had to rely upon blind luck. There was no way he could deal with the mine from within the sub. He could only sail on at the lowest possible speed, hoping that if the sub's hull struck one of the mine's horns, it would do so gently, failing to activate the charge which would rip the guts out of the underwater craft.

Number one looked at de Vere's face, now grey with fear. De Vere pulled himself together. 'Well, at least we'll all make handsome corpses,' he said, suddenly smiling, though he had never felt less like smiling in all his life. 'All right, we can't go back really, so let's go forward. Number one. Both ahead – dead slow.'

Chalky White, the crew's cockney comedian, broke the tension by crossing himself and intoning solemnly in a gravelike voice, 'For what we are about to receive, may the good Lord make us truly thankful.'

De Vere could have kissed him.

Slowly, very slowly, with every man tensed for the explosion that could come at any moment and send the submarine to the bottom of the channel for ever, the craft pressed on. Desperately, nerves tingling electrically, de Vere pressed his eyes to the periscope, turning up the amplifier so that his range was magnified and enhanced, searching for the first sign of those deadly infernal machines that he and his crew passionately despised.

But luck was on their side.

For an instant, he couldn't believe his own eyes. Then he knew that he wasn't seeing things. He had run right into a small fleet of fishing boats, the typical shrimping craft of the Frisian coast: small, with red sails, trawling the customary lopsided net behind them. But that wasn't all. The half a dozen or so boats were heading straight for him into the minefield and it was clear that they weren't going to stop when they came level with the block ship. They were going to proceed even further out.

De Vere reacted immediately, realising instantly that he could use the German small craft to his own advantage. 'Stop engines,' he commanded. Then he shouted, 'Down periscope.'

'What?' his number two commenced.

De Vere held up his hand for immediate silence. 'Silent running,' he hissed urgently. 'Every man on listening watch. A group of Hun fishing boats—' He didn't finish his words. For he could already hear the steady hard throb-throb of ancient engines approaching over his head. The Huns were almost on top of them...

'We want a body, Lieutenant,' the Flag Officer at Harwich had announced, as if he made statements of that nature every day. 'More than one, if possible.'

'Yes sir, I understand,' de Vere had replied, though of course he hadn't understood one tiny little bit. Two hours before, just after entering the naval docks, at Harwich, with not a kill to his name after a two-week patrol in the Atlantic and North Sea, he had been summoned to go straight off to the Admiral's HQ. As he shaved off his pathetic beard and struggled into his uniform, he had told himself that he was in for a rocket. This was the second fighting patrol from which he had returned without a 'kill' to his name. They might even give him the boot, he thought, and send him down south for further training. Such things did happen. Christ, they might even keep him at HQ!

But the Flag Officer, very grand, whose broad chest was heavy with the ribbons of the Old War, had soon enlightened him that he was being sent on another mission almost immediately. 'Refuel, re-victual and give the men a twenty-four hour shore leave – local – before you set off again, my lad,' the Flag Officer had said.

'Yes sir,' de Vere had managed to stutter. 'All a bit sudden, if I may say so, sir.'

'You may, de Vere,' the other officer in the room had said in his booming hail-fellow-well-met fashion. 'But the signal's just come in from the Admiralty and I think I know who's behind their Lordships on this one,' he lowered that overloud voice of his, 'Winnie himself,' he confided.

The submarine commander had been impressed. Churchill, the Prime Minister was well known for poking his nose into service affairs – a lot of officers disliked him on that account – but the younger ranks knew that 'Winnie' only did so when he saw slackness and slowness in seizing an opportunity to hurt the Hun.

'Naturally you'll want to know where the fire is, de Vere?'

He had nodded numbly, still too confused by the reference to Churchill to be able to think straight.

'I'll tell you. We've gone and lost the bloody Hun surface fleet.' The Flag Officer had looked through the spume-dirtied window of his office at the estuary – packed with destroyers and cruisers – as if he half expected the German fleet to come sailing up at any moment. 'Careless, you might admit. It was all the fault of those Brylcreem boys of the RAF. But no matter. We've lost 'em and you're gonna find 'em again for us.'

'Me, sir?' de Vere had stuttered.

'Yes, you sir.' the Flag Officer had snapped back, adding swiftly, as if time were of the essence, 'We want bodies, de Vere – and you're getting those bodies for us. After all, yours is the only sub available with such a shallow draught...'

Later Lieutenant de Vere told himself that he hadn't been picked to enter the Baltic because HMS *Defiant* had such a shallow draught. No, he'd been selected because if anyone was expendable, it was de Vere's *Defiant*, the only sub in the command which hadn't yet made a kill...

De Vere took one last glance through the periscope at the little fishing fleet. In the rear craft, the one he had already selected in his mind, a bearded fellow was throwing fish bits overboard. All about him the gulls cawed and pleaded in a flapping, whirling angry cloud of white. Then the periscope was down and, at the hydrophones, the operators tensed, ready to pick up the sounds from above. De Vere started to count the minutes.

In the submarine, all was silent save for the soft hum of the electric generators which powered the lighting. The men were tense. Their faces seemed to be greased, as if with oil. At their desk the two hydrophone operators seemed to be the only crew members to be alive, as they moved, clamping their earphones more tightly to their shaven skulls, delicately adjusting their instruments. But the crew no longer needed their services to warn the boat that the German fishing craft were approaching. They could hear the steady throb of their props as they grew ever closer.

Now de Vere's mind raced at full speed, as he thought out his plan. He'd position the *Defiant* between the block ship and the little fleet, using the fishing boats as protection in the hope that the block ship wouldn't open fire in case its shells struck then. Then he'd surface, grab the 'bodies' and do a crash dive. For in these shallows – where a submarine was always clearly outlined from the air – the *Defiant* wouldn't stand much chance if there were an aerial attack. Everything now depended upon split-second timing and the *Defiant*'s ability to do a quick bunk. His plan firm, de Vere started to issue his orders to his number one.

At the desks, the leading seaman in charge of the hydrophones sang out – 'Screws directly ahead, sir ... bearing...' – startling de Vere a little.

De Vere was no longer listening. He started to count the seconds as the screws' swishing noise started to fade and then he rapped, 'Up periscope.' The operation was on.

Two

All hell was let loose.

The fishermen hadn't been fooled. As soon as the sub had surfaced, they had reacted. With surprising speed for middle-aged men, laden down with heavy clothing and bad weather gear. Almost as soon as de Vere's number one, armed, with – of all things – a naval cutlass, started to swing himself over the side of the fishing boat, followed by Chalky White, toting a Thompson sub-machine gun, the bigger of the two Germans had grabbed an old-fashioned flare gun and, even before the number one had been able to warn him against retaliating in his pathetic German, the fisherman had fired it off.

It had exploded over their heads, In an instant they had been bathed in a glowing blood-red light. Chalky White hadn't hesi-tated. He pressed the trigger of his Tommy gun. The Germans who had fired the flare, shrieked. Blood erupted from what seemed to be a series of red buttonholes, stitched across the front of their chests. Next moment, arms flailing wildly, one of the Germans had gone over the side. He didn't come up. And the other German raised his arms in surrender.

Just in time. The block ship had understood the situation instantly. Tracers zipped across the intervening distance in a lethal morse. Slugs howled off the submarine's hull like heavy tropical rain on a tin roof. Chalky White slammed the butt of his weapon into the German's back. The man nearly fell into the clutches of the *Defiant*'s waiting sailors. An instant later, its klaxon making an ear-splitting sound, the submarine was performing a crash dive just as the block ship's heavy guns opened up...

The alarm was raised all over the north of Germany. At HQ they had almost immediately tumbled to what the Tommies were about. One didn't send a submarine to snatch the crew of a humble Cuxhaven fishing boat, did one? The Tommies were after bigger fish and the submarine had to be stopped before it got back to its base to report. And the staff at Wilhelmshaven Naval HQ knew that the submariners on the run wouldn't break radio silence during their flight across the North Sea; they wouldn't reach their base if they did.

All air bases from Jever on the Frisian coast

to Fuhlsbuttel, just outside Hamburg were put on red alert. Everywhere, the search planes took to the air. All coastal shipping off occupied Holland and Norway to the north were ordered out. From the German naval bases at Texel, Zeebrügge and Calais, the coastal craft, sub-chasers, mine-sweepers, E-boats – anything that could be sent to sea swiftly – were alerted for immediate operational duty. It seemed as if the whole of the German Forces were now working to knock out one obsolescent British submarine...

While the kidnapped German fisherman slept in a makeshift bunk between the aft torpedo tubes, drugged to the world – for he had refused to settle down and had been getting on the crew's already taut nerves – de Vere steered a course for home. Already Harwich had offered its congratulations – HQ had picked up the German signals about the kidnapping – and had warned de Vere that from now on he had to keep total radio silence: the Huns were out gunning for him everywhere.

It was clear from the hydrophone operators' readings that Harwich had been right. The operators had been picking up enemy ships all the time, while they had stuck close to the occupied Dutch Frisian islands. The radio operator had reported similar findings. 'The air waves are full of Jerry messages, sir,'

108

he had informed a pale, anxious de Vere in his broad Yorkshire accent. 'Yon buggers are out to get us. We're gonna have to be reet jammy to dodge the squareheads this time, sir.'

Silently de Vere agreed. They *were* going to have to be 'reet jammy'. Still he kept on doggedly, encouraged by the efforts of his young crew. Though their nerves stretched to the limit de Vere knew his 'matelots' wouldn't let him down.

They had just left the Dutch territorial waters off the island of Texel, happy that no one at that great German naval base had picked them up, when the leading hand, hydrophone operator lifted up one earphone and reported urgently that 'Bridge, we've got a contact!'

Swiftly de Vere nodded to his number one to take over and bound to where the pale-faced sweat-lathered operator was again listening intently, trying to pick up more details of the strange screws.

De Vere waited, biting his bottom lip, for he would have dearly loved to ask what the operator had heard. But he forced himself to bide his time. While he waited he flung a glance at the depth meter. One hundred and ten! Deep, but not deep enough.

'There you are, sir,' the operator announced, as if he had achieved some fearsome but personal triumph. 'It's a Jerry.'

De Vere didn't argue. Only a Hun would be in these waters and even if it weren't a naval vessel, it would be under German control. He reacted immediately. 'Stop both,' he commanded quietly. 'Silent running. No noise. Let's listen.'

The crew needed no urging. They froze at their posts, hardly daring to breathe.

The cat-and-mouse game had commenced. The side which kept its cool, its nerve the longest would win. Thus they waited as the sound of the screws above grew louder and louder. But strangely enough, as that sound rose to a crescendo, a dull menacing thunder, all that de Vere seemed to hear was the steady drip-drip of a minor leak somewhere in the bulkhead.

'Large vessel,' the operator hissed. 'Twin set of screws. Bearing a red seven-five. Could be a destroyer.'

De Vere cursed inwardly. If it was a seven-five, they were in for trouble. But his tense young face revealed nothing to the crew who were watching him intently. For, although he wasn't the best submarine commander in the world, he had learned one thing since he had taken over his own command: panic in a sub under attack starts at the top with the skipper.

Now the screws were almost directly

above. De Vere was sweating freely. He could feel the back of his old school soccer shirt, which he wore on patrols, damp with sweat. For he knew what would come now if they had been spotted and somehow he thought they had. The enemy would have no mercy. They'd drop a diamond pattern of depth charges. If they exploded close enough to the old *Defiant*, she'd twist and groan as if the hull were being wrung like some washer-woman wringing out her laundry.

Thereafter the pressure waves would force the deck plates to jump. Glass dials would splinter. Glass would zip through the boat frighteningly – lethally. Packing and gaskets would fracture. Water would start trickling in. You'd pray fervently that it would not turn into a flood. For you wouldn't dare to start the pumps because they'd give away your position on the seabed.

Then you'd sit at the bottom. You'd be lathered in sweat. You'd gasp for breath like some poor old asthmatic fart in the throes of a final attack. The air would get fouler by the minute. The men would become snappy and ill-tempered. The whole vile atmosphere of the trapped sub would become even worse. And so the litany of horrors would escalate. De Vere forced a weary smile. No wonder most submarine skippers ended up drunks – or in the looney bin.

The screws were drowning out every other sound, even that of the squeaking bulkhead. Fast turbines. De Vere recognised the whine. A destroyer – or destroyers – moving at speed.

Noiselessly de Vere began to count. To time the crossing of the sub by the craft above. Would the enemy ship miss them. Forcing him to measure out the timing, he went on ... *three ... four ... five ... six...*

Wildly, he grabbed for a stanchion, as the depth charges exploded all about the *Defiant*. It was buffeted from side to side like a toy boat, as if struck by a gigantic fist. The lights went out. Next moment they flickered back on again to reveal a scene of absolute chaos. The whole interior of the boat was in total confusion. But the crew had no time to concern themselves with the mess. There were more depth charges coming down.

Again the *Defiant* was slammed back and forth effortlessly. Dials popped. Plates sprang leaks. One of the batteries was flooded. Suddenly noxious biting gas started to escape into the hull. Men started to cough furiously. But there was no end to the torture. More and more of the deadly high explosive eggs came floating down to explode all about the *Defiant*. She lurched alarmingly. She began to sink. For one terrible moment, de Vere thought she was going down for good. But to everyone's surprise, she righted herself and remained there, trembling, it seemed, like some drenched frightened dog just pulled out of a stream and saved from an early death.

And then the screws had gone. At their desks, the hydrophone operators slumped, heads bent, temporarily exhausted. They were the only ones to move. The rest remained as they were, as if they were already dead, frozen into a grotesque waxwork of death for eternity. But all were listening ... listening ... listening. Was that it? Or were their torturers not satisfied? Would they come back for another run of depth charging: one that could only spell the doom of the *Defiant*?

'*Na und?*' Raeder demanded. Behind, holding the telephone attachment, Doenitz listened for the staff officer's reply. For him it was a matter of total unconcern. One way or the other Raeder was going to have to lose his capital ships and make way for his, Doenitz's war winners: his 'grey wolves', the underwater killers of the U-boat Service.

The staff officer hesitated. 'We can't be sure, *Herr Grossadmiral*,' he answered Raeder's query hesitantly. 'You never can be in these matters—'

'Don't play me for a damned fool, Commander,' Raeder interrupted the officer at the other end of the line with, for him, un-accustomed rudeness. Doenitz told himself Old Wheels was losing his nerve. 'I know about such things. Any tell-tale signs of a sinking? You know, Commander – oil slick, bodies, bits of clothing, etc?'

Still the man at the other end was hesitant. Waiting for his answer, an equally impatient Doenitz told himself, 'Come on, man, piss or get off the pot, won't you?'

Finally the staff officer spoke. 'We think, *Herr Grossadmiral*, that the attack *must* have been successful. There has been no radio traffic between the submarine and the English authorities, which is unusual for the English who foolishly tend to give their position away by—'

'Get on with it,' Raeder said gruffly.

'Sorry, sir. Most importantly, the English have not alerted any of their forward air force bases in Scotland, which they do when they feel there is a need to give protection and cover to one of their vessels which is damaged or in danger.' His voice trailed away to nothing, as if he had said all he was going to say.

Raeder flashed Doenitz a look of enquiry. Doenitz considered for a moment. The staff officer, pompous fool as he seemed to be over the phone, had a case. The English were

114

not observing standard operating procedure when one of their boats was in trouble. He nodded to indicate that he felt that the Tommy sub had been sunk.

Raeder hesitated briefly. For a change and for such an old man, Doenitz couldn't help thinking, he made his decision quickly. 'All right, Commander,' he snapped, 'let's assume that the English submarine has been sunk. For the time being the English will be working blind. But I want maximum effort on radio traffic and naval shipping movements on the island. Anything suspicious, especially at Scapa Flow,' Raeder meant the home of the Royal Navy's Home Fleet, 'and I want to know immediately. *Klar*?'

'*Klar, Herr Grossadmiral,*' the answer came promptly.

'All right, that's it for the time being.'

With a clearly audible sigh of relief, the Commander at the other end put the phone down and Raeder, turning to Doenitz, asked, 'Well, do you think I did the right thing, Doenitz?'

'Yes,' Doenitz answered without the slightest hesitation. After all, things were going according to his plan. When things went wrong, the Führer wouldn't blame him. Old Wheels would be the one who'd get the Führer's thickest cigar.

Raeder frowned, his mind seemingly elsewhere. 'So the Fleet will assemble at Danzig,' he said after a few moments of reflection. 'We won't have much time. The Führer won't give us much time. Naturally.' He laughed a little bitterly. 'But when has the Führer had much time for our surface fleet?'

Doenitz didn't comment.

Raeder went on with, 'So, as soon as the weather provides the cover we need, our ships will make a run for the enemy. Once we're out of the Baltic and into the open sea, I don't think our vessels can be stopped. The English might out-number us, but we have the fastest, most modern and most powerful ships in the whole world. Theirs are the outmoded products of the Old War.' Raeder beamed with sudden pride at the other admiral.

Doenitz allowed him his moment of pride. Raeder's days were numbered. Let him live in his dream world for a little longer. 'Yes, *Herr Grossadmiral*,' he answered dutifully, but without conviction. 'As long as we can keep the Tommies unaware of our intentions until you are clear of the Baltic narrows, I think, sir, that you will win a battle that will make the name of the new German High Sea Fleet ring round the world, and,' he added, with a certain underlining malice, 'please the Führer as well.'

'Yes, yes,' Raeder said hurriedly, his smile vanishing. 'That is vital ... we must keep the Führer happy, must we not?'

Thus, they parted, the past and the future. Raeder would achieve his great victory, but in the end it would turn to ashes, just as Doenitz had predicted. And Gestapo Müller, watching them from his temporary office in the old German Hansa town of Danzig, told himself, as the two officers parted to their waiting staff cars, that they were both already ghosts: symbols of Hitler's vaunted '1,000-Year Reich', which wouldn't last out the decade.

Three

'Elena,' the old crone had cried as her visitor had fallen to the floor next to the door, revealing a mass of gold-blonde hair. Suddenly, the old lady's fear vanished. She turned on Savage, her face flushed with anger. 'You are a bad one, Englishman!' she shrieked, wagging her long dirty forefinger at him furiously. Behind her the frying pan started to smoke blue. A smell of burning permeated the air. 'Why did you do that? Englishman, you will never have any luck in this world, striking women like that,' she stared down at the startled young woman in a long grey Polish greatcoat that couldn't quite hide her shapely figure. 'You are accursed...'

Savage had hardly been able to understand the angry flow of words. But he had experienced a *frisson* of fear. He couldn't understand why. But there had been something uncanny about the old woman as she had stood, rheumy old eyes blazing, her outstretched talon trembling like some medieval witch's in a fairy-tale.

'*Matka*,' the blonde woman on the floor said, raising herself and holding out one hand towards the furious old crone as if attempting to calm her, '*Dobje ... dobje ... je dobje...*'

When Savage had first arrived at Weser-timke POW camp, there had been a few captive Polish naval officers and Savage had recognised the sound of the Slavic language, though he didn't understand the meaning of the words. The realisation surprised him and he soon forgot the fear that the crone had occasioned a moment before.

The old woman was of Polish origin herself, one of those labelled contemptuously by their fellow Germans as '*Wasserpolacken*', water Poles: a mixture of German and Pole, from the former border area between the two countries. The crone – Olga Schmidt – had lost her husband in the first months of the war and had continued to keep farming with the aid of her teenage son. He had now been called up by the *Wehrmacht* and, in his place, she had been given Elena Warzawa, a former student from the capital, Warsaw, whose name she bore. They had struck up a relationship which went much further than that of mistress and maid. Indeed, as Elena had eventually told Savage in her hesitant mixture of German and school English, 'She is like *Oma* ... grandmother, you say ... I look for her ... she look for me ... Understand ... *Verstanden?*'

'*Verstanden*,' he had agreed.

And over the next few days, as Savage's suspicions about the two women had weakened, he had begun to understand a lot about the disparate pair: the old one had lost her 'Emil', as she called her dead husband who had been lost in the September 1939 campaign against Poland; and Elena had paid the price of defeat. She had been transported from her middle-class home in the Polish capital to this run-down, remote farmhouse to become, as far as the local Nazis were concerned, little more than a third-class citizen, a slave labourer and Slavic sub-human, who any German could use – and abuse – in any way he or she preferred. Her beautiful body no longer belonged to her, but to the Nazi state, which had a right to it until that body no longer functioned. As Elena had once said bitterly to Savage, 'I ... animal ... just animal.' And he had known all too well what she had meant.

Savage and Elena became lovers.

The crone usually went to bed with the chickens, as she phrased it. The girl, Elena, usually read on, trying to improve her German till her eyes closed and she fell asleep. Savage, for his part, found sleep difficult.

The old woman and Elena worked hard all day, trying to keep the farm going on their labour. But Savage had been ordered by the Polish girl not to show himself during daylight hours. The result was that he wasn't as physically tired as they were.

So, one day it was with a sudden start that Savage heard the soft creak on the rickety wooden ladder which led up to the straw-filled barn above the pigs in which he slept. Had he been discovered? Hurriedly he made a grab for the sawn-off pick-handle, his only weapon; for a moment he felt as he had done when he had escaped from the POW camp, vowing to himself that he wouldn't be taken again without putting up a fight.

He lay there tensely, besides his makeshift bunk in the straw, a primitive weapon gripped in a hand that was now sweaty and hot. The footsteps, soft and hesitant, came ever nearer. Savage held his breath, ready to spring forward and deal with the intruder – whoever he was – the moment his head appeared above the trap that led into the loft.

Abruptly, he relaxed. In the yellow glare of a storm lantern, her face was revealed, framed by that lovely blonde hair, hanging loose now. During the daylight hours when she worked outside, Elena kept her hair tightly concealed beneath an old workman's cap so that, from a distance, she looked like another man to any inquisitive German male. Her figure, too, was clearly visible beneath the old crone's thin, well-worn nightgown. 'You!' he exclaimed.

She smiled at him a little nervously with those excellent white teeth of hers, 'Who you think?'

Savage, normally so taut and unsmiling, now grinned at her words. Yes, who could he have expected? Certainly not the old crone. 'Come,' he ordered and, dropping his weapon, indicated that she should sit on the blanket spread out over the rough hay and straw.

She hesitated. But only for a moment. She sat down a little carelessly. He caught a glimpse of inner thigh and the golden fuzz above. His heartbeat quickened. He had almost forgotten what it was like to go with a woman. He felt himself go red. But if Elena noticed, she made no comment. Instead she said, 'Come closer, it is cold here.'

He did so. The heat from the body, naked beneath the thin shift, seemed almost too hot to bear. He shivered and she snuggled even closer to him, so that he could feel the warm curve of her left breast close to him, so much so that his heart began racing once more. He felt it was moving so fast that it might well burst out of his ribcage at any moment.

Thus they crouched there in the barn, with the wind howling outside and the rats scrabbling in the shadows, both wreathed in a strange tense silence, the lantern casting their shadow in magnified distortion on the sloping wall, trembling and flickering as the wind caught the candle's flame the lantern.

Words came slowly ... with difficulty. Language was not only the problem; the strangeness of the situation – two strangers thrown up by the tide of war and having to resolve a personal conflict – was also against them.

But in the end, it was not the words that solved their dilemma – it was action. Suddenly without explanation, they felt into each other's arms with a kind of sob of mutual relief. He could feel Elena's heart beating furiously underneath the thin worn material. She, for her part, ran her work-worn fingers through his cropped hair, as if she were feeling the head of a beloved child, sobbing – tears of passion, joy, relief...

Later, much later, he told her his plans, as best he could. He knew he could trust her implicitly. After all, she had sacrificed her virginal body to him, giving all of herself, without hesitation, demands or reservations. Never before in his life had he ever experienced a woman who could be so sensual, so passionate and, yet, at the same time, so innocent.

She listened intently, head cocked to one side, hair askew, as if she was concentrating her whole being on his tale, not wishing to miss a single word. When Savage had finished telling Elena of his plans, she stared down at him, eyes full of love and concern, exposing her lovely breasts. Savage almost felt as if he should reach up and take one of her big dark nipples into his mouth.

'You must go one day?' she asked finally in a little voice.

He nodded, but added no explanation.

'It is the war?'

'Yes, the war,' he answered as if that in itself was explanation enough. And it was. It was always the war. For years now, Savage thought, the war had been sufficient explanation – and excuse – for everything.

She nodded solemnly, as if she finally understood, and was not prepared to object to the simplistic justification he had given for his intentions and what had happened to her own tragic homeland. A long way off a clock chimed three. Otherwise all was silent – even the wind had died down. They could have been the last living people in the whole world.

Towards dawn, Elena came to him again. This time she was not the passionate virgin of the first time. This time she was a woman full of greed and sexuality, who knew what she wanted and was prepared to take it. Her hands scratched and tore at his skinny, but muscular body. She whispered and moaned in her native language. She kissed him time and time again, her cunning little pink tongue sliding in and out of his hard gaping mouth so that he was so aroused he had the devil of a time containing himself.

Over and over again, he thrust his throbbing swollen loins against her. She responded feverishly, her lithe naked young body lathered in sweat. But when he tried to enter her she pushed him away almost angrily, as if she wanted to prolong this fervent, burning-hot sexual ritual for ever.

Finally, Elena could no longer resist and Savage thrust the tip of his aching penis into her. She squealed. She wriggled furiously. He couldn't hold back any more and grunting like an animal, he thrust himself deep into her. Elena's spine arched like the string of a taut bow. Next moment she was jerking herself back and forth with complete abandon, her teeth gritted, too, her eyes blank, savouring the cruel pillar of flesh, which seemed to be penetrating the innermost of her pleasure-racked body...

Two days later, with the old crone sobbing bitterly at the door, as if her very heart was broken, the lovers set out bravely into the dangerous unknown. Every man's hand was against them. But it didn't matter. They were in love and their love knew no fear, as long as they were together. When they were gone, the old crone dried her eyes on the end of her apron, crossed herself quickly and hobbled inside. With an air of finality, she slammed the door close behind her. They hadn't a chance, she knew that already.

Four

Furtively, the lovers crept through the evening fog down a little country path. From the heights of the Elbe village of Geesthacht, it led to the river itself. Traffic on the Elbe had died down now. Further up the river, the mournful wail of a ship's foghorn and muted throb of an engine was heard. But most of the bargees, Savage reasoned, would already be in the waterside *Kneipen*, tossing back the local *lutt un lutt*, a dialect name for a small glass of schnapps followed by a small beer chaser.

They came to the towpath. Savage indicated the girl should stop. She did so immediately. Her reactions were more like a man's, he told himself. Elena knew they were in constant danger, but she didn't let it show. They crouched and stared at the dim outline of the railway bridge beyond the road, both of which spanned the Elbe. For a few minutes Savage thought they were deserted, unguarded. But then he detected the smell of a burning match. Someone had lit a cigarette on the road bridge, and it could only be a guard.

Savage nodded to Elena and she silently acknowledged him, indicating that she had noticed the sulphurous smell too.

He peered harder. There was no sign of a sentry on the railway bridge. Savage bit his bottom lip. Back in the camp they had given a great deal of study to the Germany road-and-rail system. The prisoners agreed that *all* bridges were guarded, so he would have to assume that the railway bridge would be guarded, too, but not as well as the road, where there was constant traffic. Besides the traffic that passed over it mainly went to Berlin, but there was a local line on the other side branching to the north and the ports of the Baltic – Lübeck, Travemünde, Wismar, etc., only thirty odd miles away. That was the line they were going to take.

He looked at the girl. Her face was shrouded, but he sensed that she was ready to go, to tackle everything, though she knew she faced a concentration camp or worse if they were captured. He'd suffer only a return to Wesertimke and a month in the cooler, at the most, on bread and water. For a moment, he thought he should tell her she'd done enough and should return to the old crone's farm while she was still safe. But then he realised she wouldn't obey him. Her love was overpowering. She wanted to be with him to the very end, whatever the outcome.

Swiftly he outlined his plan and then, pressing her cold hand, whispered, 'We'll do it, Elena.'

'*Natürlich*,' she answered in German returning the pressure. '*Kein problem.*'

'*Kein problem*,' he agreed in the same language, for they had agreed to speak German now, however badly. It was less suspicious.

Five minutes later, they were cautiously edging their way down the towpath, feeling the damp cold of the fog as it rose from the great inland river and wreathed about their legs. All was silent now. If there were bargees up in the inns on the heights above, they were remarkably silent. Perhaps they were stuffing themselves with what in slang they called 'fart soup', a potent mixture of peas and sausages. But silent as the little riverside village above them was, there was no denying that the sentry on the road bridge to their right was active enough. They could hear the stamp of his steel-shod boots on the tarmac, as he paced out his beat as stiffly as if he were personally guarding the Führer in Berlin.

Still, Savage told himself, they'd be able to skirt his red-and-white striped sentry box and the similarly coloured road pole, now hung with a dim-red lantern to warn approaching vehicles that they had to stop to be checked before they could continue their journey on the country road which led to Luneburg some thirty miles away.

Savage paused again.

Before them, some twenty yards away, lay the entrance to the side of the railway bridge. Marked by a huge metal sign a kind of low latticed door presumably used by plate-layers and other railwaymen to enter and check the bridge and brains. He indicated the sign. '*Da*,' he said.

'*Ja*,' she whispered back. That was the way they'd enter the bridge.

Crouched low, their gaze fixed almost hypnotically on the red glow of the unsuspecting sentry's cigarette, they crept gingerly towards the entrance of the railway bridge. Now there was no sound save the gentle movements of the dark water lapping against the bridge's support and the muffled tread of the sentry, alone with his thoughts. They reached the iron gate. With caution, Savage attempted to open it. It was stuck. He cursed under his breath. The damned thing was bolted. He prayed it wasn't padlocked as well. It wasn't. He breathed a sigh of relief. Then he set about drawing back the bolt. Elena tensed at his side, throwing glances at the red glimmer, as he drew back the rusty catch inch by inch.

It seemed to make a devil of a noise. Savage thought that Hitler could hear the the rusty squeak all the way off in Berlin. He felt a cold bead of sweat trickle down the small of his back. But still the sentry continued to walk his beat, stolidly.

'Nearly done,' Savage whispered, hardly recognising his own voice. Elena nodded, not trusting herself to speak. Finally he'd done it and straightened, gasping, as if he had just run a race. For a moment he couldn't proceed any further. His right hand was shaking violently with the tension. Then she nudged him urgently. From the slope opposite, heading down from Geesthacht towards the river, there came the sound of a car negotiating the steep curve. It was someone connected with the sentry. Savage knew that instinctively. Perhaps it was the guard commander coming to inspect or change sentries.

Savage felt the adrenalin streaming through his veins. There was no time to lose. He tugged at the gate. It didn't move. The damned thing had rusted in place. He had no time to reason the whys and wherefores. The car was nearly round the bend. In a minute its blacked-out headlights would sweep their end of the railway bridge. He tugged hard. The gate flew open with a rusty squeak that sounded to him like a knell of doom.

Next moment the car swept round the corner. Its beam flashed upon them. The sentry challenged, '*Halt wer da?*' For a moment they were blinded, outlined a stark black, pinned down in the circle of light, clearly up to no good. The sentry must have thought so, for he cried, '*Halt ... stehenbleiben oder ich schiesse...*' and, without waiting to see whether they would stop or not, he fired.

The sudden shot galvanised the two fugitives into action. With a grunt, Savage pushed the girl through the gate on to the sleepers and the line. 'Run,' he yelled as the sentry's bullet howled frighteningly off the iron stanchion near his head. Next moment, he had followed her through and was running all out and awkwardly towards the other end of the railway bridge.

The car started again. There was a screech of tyres. Shots followed. Cries of rage. Again, the searchlight beam of the car's headlights caught up with them, as other men in the car now joined in the wild firing. Desperately, the two of them zig-zagged the best they could between the sleepers. More than once a bullet cut the air just by them, as they raced for the cover of the far side, arms working like pistons, breath coming in harsh hectic gasps.

Next to him, the girl kept up. She needed no encouragement. If she were afraid, Savage thought, she didn't show it. She was a good trooper, ready for anything. But once again, he realised just how much was at stake for her. If she were caught now, there would only be one punishment – death.

Behind them, though they couldn't see it, the new arrivals were setting up a machine gun, with more accuracy and distance than that of the German rifle, to fire the length of the bridge.

But if they couldn't see what the enemy was up to, they were aware that if they didn't make the slight bend and the dark shadows beyond, they were going to die – *soon*.

Startlingly, frighteningly, the machine gun opened up. A high-pitched hysterical burst. White tracer zipped all about them. It sliced the leaves from the trees in a green rain. Slugs howled off the rails. Splinters flew everywhere. The air seemed filled with lethal, burning, flying, steel.

The girl stumbled. 'Elena!' he yelled in absolute, overwhelming panic. He grabbed for her. Too late. Next instant she had pitched over the side of the embankment, disappearing into the darkness beyond and he was following her into the unknown in a shower of gravel and earth...

★ ★ ★

Müller looked up from the report and nodded, as if confirming something to himself. Down below in the courtyard of the Prinz Albrecht Gestapo HQ, Berlin, they were shooting the latest two POWs who had been recaptured the night before. They were both naval officers, the kind that Müller needed for his plan, but they were useless to him now; they had been in the custody of the local military – where they had been recaptured – too long. Scores of soldiers and perhaps the same number of rubber-necked gawping civilians had seen them in that time. Even the Gestapo couldn't prevent that number of ordinary German citizens from relating what they had seen; so the POWs were now hopelessly compromised. They had to be eradicated.

He sniffed as the Gestapo officials below got on with their awkward task. It would have been easier if they had been able to tie them to a post and shoot them dead. But that was impossible. The Swiss cuckoo-clock bastards of the Red Cross, who would have to certify that the Tommies had been shot while trying to escape, would want to see irregular wounds somewhere in their backs. Frontal ones, as inflicted by a firing squad, would have been out of the question; they would have given the game away. He dismissed the screams, shots and angry shouts coming from below and looked at the report once more.

It was clear, he told himself, that they were on the trail of another two escapees: Royal Navy men trying to cross the Elbe and heading north for the Baltic ports.

In their haste to get across the Lauenburg railway bridge, one of the escapees had left a haversack behind. It had been dyed a darkish colour, probably with the writing ink used in POW camps. The sack was definitely of English manufacture and bore on the inside flap a name, number and what Müller had been told by one of his aides, was a naval rank. An English naval officer all right. But no further clues had been picked up by the local garrison.

He sat back and rubbed his eyes with his massive paws – the fingers covered with dark animal-like black hairs – and thought. Down below one of the escaped Tommies was being chased around the yard by the fat, panting Gestapo officials. He had been hit. Still he hopped on fearfully, knowing what would happen if he fell down or stopped, the blood arcing from his shattered calf in a bright red stream, sparkling in the early morning sunshine.

Müller sighed. What bungling, hopeless amateurs these Gestapo men were; they didn't know the first thing about real police work. He was half inclined to stand up, fling open the window and yell, 'Go for the back, man ... the broadest part of the body,' but in the end he didn't. Let them get on with it.

Müller's plan was simple: these Gestapo men would hand the escapers over to another branch of country police outside, who would know nothing of what had previously happened and who would carry out their part of the scheme. This group of Gestapo brutes would be responsible for the final part of the scene: the discovery and shooting of the escapers. Müller knew that they had to make it look real, that the marks on the corpses would convince the damned Red Cross that the Tommies were shot while trying to escape...

Müller stared a little while longer at the documents and the attached map of Mecklenburg, the area in which the two fugitives had last been sighted. He made his decision. He clicked on the switch of the intercom which connected him with his outer office. 'Heinz,' he called.

'*Standartenführer?*'

'These are going to be the two.'

'Orders, *Standartenführer?*' Heinz, the born subordinate, who would probably die in a nice comfy bed of old age – Müller cynically reflected – thought it very efficient and

136

military to answer in clipped hacked-off phrases.

'To be apprehended and arrested without any physical damage inflicted to their persons. Should any damage be done to either of them, I shall hold the officer in charge personally responsible. Clear?'

'*Klar, Standartenführer.*'

Müller clicked the switch off. The intercom went dead. For a few moments he brooded thus.

Down below they had trapped another POW. They had caught him in the small of the back. A dark red patch was spreading rapidly across his torn shirt. He wouldn't live long. Still, as all young men do, he had fought for life. But there was no chance – his hands now raised and clasped together in the classic pose of supplication, he quickly turned to face one of the officials who was going to shoot him. Lining up behind the first official were several more men, all ready, waiting to fire.

Müller told himself, watching the scene below but not really taking it in, that once he had caught and briefed the two English escapees, he would be walking on thin ice, very thin ice indeed. But it was the only way he was going to pull it off. His heavy peasant face brightened. If it all worked out as he had planned, there'd be no turning back and his place and future in the other camp (he rarely used 'Moscow') would be assured for ever. He would be the spy who had destroyed the German Fleet.

Down below, a heavy, fat Gestapo man standing behind the escaper – now bleeding but still on his knees, pleading for his life – paused. Silently, the heavy Gestapo raised his pistol. His face revealed nothing. He didn't even seem to take aim. He pressed the trigger. There was a stiffled scream of absolute agony. The boy pitched face forward, as the back of his head shattered like a lightly boiled egg struck by a heavy spoon. Hastily the killer cop stepped back to avoid the spurt of blood that might have spoiled the polish of his boots. Together with the other Gestapo executors, he stared at the corpse. It was beginning to steam – they always did for a while – like the carcasses of the beasts that Müller remembered from the Munich slaughter houses of his youth.

Müller made a little sound. It might have been a sigh; it might not have been. He bent his shaven head over his papers once more. Down below the corpse started to stiffen...

Five

It was that old POW trick of getting into the centre of a town without asking questions of the 'civvies', which was likely to be dangerous. All around Savage and the Polish girl in her ankle-length man's coat, workers streamed to the factories and shipyards. Most were on foot, but some were on bicycles, while others crowded at the tramstops, stamping their cold feet in the chill dawn air, waiting for the rickety ancient trams. All of them were as shabby as the two fugitives and all carried cheap briefcases, which didn't hold documents as they would have done in England, but flasks of cold tea and sandwiches for lunch.

Savage was waiting for the arrival of a tram that was particularly crowded indicating that it was heading for one of the central factories. Elena and Savage would follow it along the lines. To board and ride the tram would have been easier – and they were weary enough – but it wasn't a risk worth taking. In Nazi Germany, you needed damned identity documents for everything and they had none.

For the last two days, the two of them had been heading north-east using only country roads and avoiding villages wherever possible. They had food enough for yet another two days so that was no problem to eat. All the same, Savage had soon realised that by now a massive search to find them would have been launched. Ever since they had escaped at the railway bridge by the skin of their teeth, the Gestapo would have been on to them. More than once they had spotted police patrols and barricades on the main roads. Troops had been out, too, combing the countryside in long lines, beating grass and bushes, as fugitives – in the soldiers' minds – were nothing better than dangerous wild animals. Once they had nearly been discovered by a low-flying Storch reconnaissance plane, which had come in at tree-top height with its engine switched off momentarily. That had scared them and Elena, so tough and capable otherwise, had been forced to vomit with the shock. Thereafter she had not spoken for quite a while, until she had given him that brilliant, encouraging smile of hers and had whispered in German, *'Entschuldigung* – sorry...'

It was at that moment that Savage, so hard, so undemonstrative, was filled with an overwhelming sense of love. Now he knew he had done wrong to involve Elena in this unnecessary danger. All the same he knew, too, that nothing would harm her. He'd rather die than allow it.

Now they were approaching the centre of Wismar. Already he could smell that old familiar mix of gutted fish, sea, and rotting timber. They were close to the waterfront now; and now their problems would really begin. He gave Elena a little nudge and brought his forefinger to his lips, in warning. She responded immediately. She nudged him back and he knew everything would work out.

Steadily, they followed the tramlines, sticking to the ones which gleamed the most. For these were the lines which were most used.

Traffic was now getting even thicker. There were cars, mostly military, and horse-drawn carts, filled with produce from outside Wismar, going to the market. Savage spotted the *Hauptbahnhof*, which was adorned with the customary patriotic legend, *'Raeder rollen fur den Sieg'* – 'wheels roll for victory'. Savage sniffed. Not if he had his bloody way.

More and more sailors hove into view. There were those from the German Navy, no different to their matelot equivalents back in Pompey, Hull and Harwich: cocky young men, with cheeky eyes, looking at every piece of skirt, however old, as if they were there for the taking. Savage, however, was more interested in the merchant seamen, who filled the area around the main station. As they passed in their blue serge uniforms, he tried to pick up scraps of their conversation, his eyes lighting up when he heard they were speaking in Swedish. For it was a neutral Swedish ship that he was looking for this day.

Half an hour later they were in the dock area proper. It was the sort of shabby rundown area that Savage had seen in half a dozen continental ports on training cruises before the war. Here were the places that bored, thirsty, randy matelots sought out for a few hours of cheap pleasure among cheap people. Dingy bars and cafés reeking of stale beer and smoke, loud with raucous laughter and brassy music.

Here aged, raddled pros with dyed blonde hair and obscenely short skirts lounged about smoking in doorways with their bored seen-it-all-before gaze, offering their wares for a handful of coins. Barkers and pimps were there, too, trying to entice the wanderer to come inside their establishment for a quick thrill. At first their faces and mouths were full of promises but if their wares were turned down, the smiles and joviality would burn to pouts and slanging anger.

Next to Savage, Elena looked in wonder at the tawdry cheapness of it all and Savage told himself, though she had come from a great city she had probably never seen anything as seedy and sex-charged as this. No matter. These port hang-outs were dangerous too. The authorities might allow them to exist so that the sailors could get their 'heavy water' off their chests. But they wanted to control them too. Such haunts of petty crime, VD and drunken fist fights had to be patrolled regularly and any potential outbursts of trouble stamped out right from the start.

Slowly, looking like two men – for at a distance, Elena, in her trousers and heavy coat, could be taken for a man – out for a casual day, the pair sauntered down the quayside beyond the harbour entrance. No one took much notice of them, even the twin naval sentries at the gate to the harbour, checking the passes of the stream of pale-faced, tired, undernourished dock workers, hurrying to their ships. It was just another grey day in the grey middle years of a long, long war.

Savage's feet were beginning to ache. As a sailor, he wasn't used to walking long distances, but he kept on, his face revealing nothing. At his side, Elena, a head shorter, did the same. In reality, their nerves were stretched to the limit, as their eyes searched for a suitable place to spend a few hours during which they would survey the harbour, looking for Swedish ships and ways to get on to them without being spotted by the ship's police and the odd bored naval sentry on patrol.

More than once they were about to turn into what they supposed would be a place – an inn – where they might carry out their task undisturbed when something had made them turn away. They knew when something spelled danger: above one inn door was a fading sign from pre-war days announcing, *'Jüden Unerwünscht'*; in the window of another was a large poster of Hitler with the initials of the Nazi Party scribbled on it, plus a number indicating that the pub was the meeting place or the local branch of the National Socialist Workers' Party.

Savage was a little surprised – he had always thought that the North German waterfront was strictly 'red', anti-Nazi. Until Hitler's takeover of power in 1933, it had traditionally been the home of the socialist and communist parties. Still he gave no thought to the matter, but nudged Elena and the two of them hurried on without sparing either inn a second glance.

It was thus engaged that they were surprised by the sudden appearance of the fat

Schupo at the corner opposite. There was no mistaking the local policeman with his black shako, ankle-length green coat and rifle slung over his shoulder. But what really caught their attention was the clipboard he held in his right hand – and Savage didn't need a crystal ball to guess that the information on it somehow referred to them. The fat cop was obviously on the look-out for the two fugitives.

They came to a sudden stop, as the policeman turned his gaze in their direction.

What were they to do? Savage realised, a little helplessly, that if they made a sudden move, the cop would sound the alarm, which would put an end to Wismar as a way out of the Reich. But could they just stroll on, knowing that the *Schupo* would probably stop them and ask for their papers, which were non-existent? Instinctively, Savage felt in his pocket. There rested his only weapon, a very primitive one at that: an old sock filled with sand. If the worse came to the worse, it could be used as a blackjack.

Fortunately, Savage was not going to have to use the crude club on the *Schupo*, for in that very same instant, Elena nudged him hurriedly and whispered, 'Listen!' She cocked her head to one side to indicate that he should do the same.

He did so. For what seemed a long time,

145

Savage didn't recognise that something strange was happening. But eventually he heard it: as early as it was, there was music coming from all sides... *'Das Oberkommando der Wehrmacht gibt bekannt ... Es war im Monat Mai ... Heute abend spricht der Führer...'* War communiqués, cheery songs, public announcements – they were pouring out on all sides from the pear-shaped 'People's Receivers', which had, by law, to be kept on at all times so that the populace should know and appreciate what the 1,000-Year Reich was achieving for its loyal citizens.

But among all that noise, there was another tune that was definitely out of place.

For a moment, a puzzled Savage couldn't put his finger on it. But Elena soon enlightened him. Urgently, she whispered *'Die Internationale,'* just as the cop started to advance towards them with the full majesty of the law.

'Die Internationale?' Savage echoed in bewilderment. Then he got it. 'Of course,' he exploded. 'The communist...' He didn't finish. With the cop only a matter of yards away, the two of them moved into the *'Kneipe zum Hein Muck'* with apparent casualness and headed for the back of the smoke-filled room from which the anthem of the International Communist movement

was coming. Casting a look over his shoulder, Savage caught a glimpse of the cop through the window. The *Schupo* hesitated in front of the dingy seamen's pub, realising it wouldn't be wise to venture into the place, and moved on, followed by the bold sound of international communism – and good will to all men...

'You're safe,' a fat man with thick sensual red lips said, as the pair came face to face with him in the back room. 'Or as safe as you'll ever be in this accursed country.' He spat bitterly on to the sawdust floor and then took a great slug of beer from the lidded stein in front of him. His accent was strange, almost slurring. It was clear that it was not his natural accent. Was he frightened – aware that his voice might occasion a reaction in one of his listeners? Elena, wiser to these things than Savage, a native of a remote island cut off from the mores of continental Europe, had already given him one possible explanation for the man's accent. As the fat man had beckoned them into the back room, she had whispered, '*Zhid*.' A few seconds later Savage had understood the meaning of the Polish word: 'Zhid' had to mean 'Yid'. The fat man was, of all things in Nazi Germany, a Jew!

If the fat man with the sensual mouth felt it strange to be a Jew in Nazi Germany,

147

allowing the *Internationale* to be played in his waterfront pub, he didn't show it. He said in English (a pleasant surprise this time for Savage, who was straining himself by trying to converse in German all the while), 'We must not fear them. We must show them our strength.' He looked around the outer room, packed with Swedish sailors. Most of them drunk, even though it was so early the morning. 'What could that policeman do against these men? Besides they are neutral. Germany wants no trouble with Sweden. Sweden is too important.'

Surprised as he was by the strange turn of events, Savage nodded. He knew that supposedly neutral Sweden supplied Germany with most of its strategic goods.

'Ah well,' the fat man continued, smirking at them, as if he were particularly pleased with himself, for some reason known only to himself, 'We knew you and your kind would be coming this way. You English people from the camps always do.'

For the first time Elena spoke and there was note of impatient contempt in her voice, Savage thought, as she said to the fat man in German, 'Are you going to help us?'

'Yes,' he replied in the same language, though this time he didn't smirk. Savage felt he had taken a dislike to Elena; why, though, he couldn't fathom. The Jewish man clapped his hands, and, as if by magic, the barman appeared bearing a tray. On it, he had two rather unclean bowls of steaming pea soup, each containing a fat greasy sausage. There were two hunks of bread as well as half a litre of foaming beer. 'Eat first,' he said inn English, grandly waving his pudgy hand with its bitten-down fingernails at the tray, 'then talk.'

Elena and Savage didn't need a second invitation. They hadn't eaten anything warm for two days now, ever since they had left the old crone's farm. The saliva of anticipation started to dribble down the side of Savage's chin and the fat man said, *'Kinnwasser...'* then in English, 'chin water, eh?' But Savage was too busy shovelling down the soup, in between great bites of the fresh bread, to comment.

Half an hour, later they were on their way. It was almost as if the Fat Man (he still hadn't given them his name) had known they were coming and had already planned everything. They were going to be smuggled aboard the Danish freighter *Kolding*. Savage had questioned him, but the Fat Man had answered easily, almost as if he had been prepared for the question, 'The Nazis don't bother the Danes as much as they do the Swedes. After all Denmark is under German occupation. Who would want to escape from one part of Germany to another, as it were?' With an almost greasy smile on his blubbery face, he had answered his own question, with: 'Of course, the thick heads of the local customs will only be interested in the ship's manifest to Denmark. They won't bother to check the *Kolding*'s next port—'

'Which is somewhere in Sweden,' Savage had interrupted.

The Fat Man had smiled, as if he were pleased that others were as cunning as him.

Now, as they proceeded to the berth of the *Kolding*, helping to push the chandler's cart – piled high with provisions for the Danish ship – the Fat Man told them how they would go aboard with the rest of the loading crew and while the naval guards were being plied with Danish aquavit, they would be smuggled down swiftly to the anchor locker. Here they would remain while customs and immigration officials gave the ship the usual departure search, leaving that night on the tide.

The Fat Man assured them, 'I have done it successfully before, I shall do it again.' He had looked severely at the two of them, 'Obey orders – *one hundred per cent.*'

They nodded their understanding and, at that juncture, Savage would have liked to have asked him a hundred questions, but he refrained. Somehow he didn't trust the Fat

Man. Why was this man risking his neck to help them?

They continued pushing the heavy cart, one of many heading the same way to the berths and the waiting ships.

Six

If Lieutenant de Vere had been an emotional man, he would have blubbed. Still he was moved. After two patrols, which had been total washouts, he was now entering Harwich to the cheers of his comrades in the rest of the Twentieth Submarine Flotilla, who lined the decks of their lean deadly grey craft and waved their hats, while further off, the cruisers of the Light Squadron sounded their horns and sirens, too.

'Holy cow,' de Vere called to his second-in-command, as the two of them stood proudly in the conning tower of the *Defiant*, with the crew in their best white jumpers lining the deck below, 'you'd ruddy well think we'd sunk the ruddy *Bismarck* itself. What a carry on.'

'What a carry on indeed, sir,' his number one called back, as the gulls cawed and cried around the little craft, as if they, too, were joining in the welcome for the battered sub, its hide scratched a bright silver with near misses from the depth charges.

Only one member of those present on the deck that cold April morning was unhappy with the reception the submarine was receiving. It was the kidnapped shrimp fisherman, standing at the base of the conning tower under the watchful eye of an armed petty officer, muttering to himself in Frisian dialect about who was going to boil his shrimp now that he had been abducted by these 'English naval gangsters'.

An hour later, he was facing a whole panel of the 'English naval gangsters', who threw pointed questions at him without cease, speaking fluent German and, in one case, actually speaking with his own Frisian tongue. Outside in the office of the Flag Officer Harwich, de Vere was similarly having to submit to a barrage of questions, posed by an somewhat effete, yet broken-nosed Old Etonian, masquerading as a lieutenant-commander in Naval Intelligence. Fleming, an officer in the 'Wavy Navy', had apparently come down from London specifically to take the prisoner back with him and find out the circumstances of his capture.

Fleming quizzed de Vere like some old salt straight off the quarterdeck of a cruiser, say, who had been sailing the seven seas since Nelson's day, instead of being a temporary officer, who had probably learned all he would ever know about seamanship from weekends of 'mucking about' in small boats in the Solent before the war, complete with Pimm's Cup and cucumber sandwiches.

As patiently as he could, de Vere answered the Old Etonian's questions, while the latter chain-smoked expensive hand-rolled cigarettes through a holder, looking rather like – de Vere couldn't help thinking – a not so camp Noel Coward. Ian Fleming, ex-journalist and future writer, currently a key member of Room 39 – the centre of Naval Intelligence in the Admiralty – was anything but a weed.

Fleming was out to make a career while in the Navy, enjoying every minute of the daily espionage games in which he was involved. It was a purely personal matter. Patriotism and the successful outcome of the war were not his first priorities. Fleming had more personal ambitions. Everything the war had forced upon him was to be stored up in his mind for future reference.

Finally Commander Fleming had had enough. He knew he had obtained all the information he was going to get from the young sub commander. But before he left for London with the prisoner and his escort, he chanced a final question. 'Lieutenant de Vere,' he said, 'what do you think the Hun surface fleet will do now?'

De Vere was surprised. He didn't think

Lieutenant-Commander Ian Fleming would think him capable of having an original idea in his head. Still he answered promptly enough, 'There's only one thing the Jerries can do now, sir.'

'And that is?' Ian Fleming narrowed his eyes to slits and let the blue cigarette smoke curl around them. It was one of his favourite poses. It made him appear very moody, mysterious and damnably attractive to the opposite sex.

'Come out.'

'Why?'

'Because we seem to have driven them from the safest anchorage in the Baltic, well protected by flak, flyboys and the like. They wouldn't last long in any of the other Baltic ports once we've twigged where they're located.'

'You mean bomb them out of the harbour?'

'Exactly, sir.' De Vere was getting tired of being quizzed: Fleming picking his brains without letting on why.

Fleming savoured de Vere's answer for a few moments. 'And then?' he asked finally.

De Vere shrugged his shoulders carelessly. 'Search me, sir. You know the Hun? He has a mind of his own that works without any apparent logic.' His voice picked up. 'But of one thing you can be sure, sir.'

'And what's that, Lieutenant?' Fleming snapped, not liking the young man's snotty tone one bit – didn't he realise he was talking to a superior officer?

'When he comes out, it'll be with a bloody big bang and if we don't watch out, he'll catch us with our knickers around our ankles.'

The remark had triggered something off at the back of Fleming's mind, but he contended himself with wishing de Vere a 'good afternoon' and going out into the courtyard where the staff car was waiting to take him to Harwich Station. His brain was racing furiously...

The first class compartment of the overnight train from Harwich to London was empty. Outside, the corridor was packed with troops, squatting on their kitbags and packs, laden with rifles, steel helmets, gas masks and the like – even the rack nets in the third class carriages would he occupied by the luckier ones, trying to get a 'kip' – cursing the slowness of the wartime trains.

Fleming was totally unconcerned by the plight of the men who would do the fighting. After all, wasn't it what they were there for: to fight and die at the command of the brass hats from the War Office? But as he considered the problem of the missing German fleet, he did continue to eye the neat little

Wren, who didn't look a day over eighteen, propped up on her kitbag, legs crossed, but all the same revealing a sizeable portion of delightful black-sheathed thigh. Idly, he told himself, she'd be worth a sin or two, although she was only a common rating.

Fleming's boss, Admiral Godfrey, Chief of Naval Intelligence, was not really cut out for this kind of work – he should have been on the quarterdeck of a cruiser, not presiding over Room 39. He was out of depth there among the smart young men of naval intelligence. He had come to rely on their advice and suggestions, especially those made by Fleming – and, as Fleming knew, Godfrey had the ear of no less a person than Winston Churchill, the Prime Minister, himself. Convince Godfrey of the scheme, which was beginning to unwind in his fertile mind like the coils of some deadly snake about to strike, and Churchill might well buy it. That would mean promotion, perhaps even the good 'gong' that he coveted.

Fleming pursed his thin somewhat cruel lips, as he considered the plan, knowing that once Godfrey and Churchill had been sold the idea, their Lordships at the Admiralty would just have to do what they were bloody well told, whether they liked it or not.

Outside, the young Wren with the raven-black hair and innocent baby-blue eyes had given up trying to sleep in the crowded corridor. Instead she stared enviously into the empty compartment with its deep, red-plush cushions and seats The seats had even got frilly pre-war antimacassars on them. Now there was almost a look of longing in her eyes.

Fleming felt his lips suddenly go dry. He loved innocence in a woman. What fun it was to spoil it sexually – a game of wits, trying the virginal innocent to the limits and then beyond when she would do things that she had never even dreamed existed at the beginning of the relationship. Of all the sexual high jinks in which he had indulged himself since Eton, it had proved the most exciting.

Tentatively, Fleming, smiled at the young Wren. She blushed nicely and then after a moment smiled back a little hesitantly.

Thereafter followed a few moments of dumb play: nods, shakes of the head, a little warm waving, head shaken in refusal at the invitation to enter the compartment, a series of ever deeper blushes and then finally the nod of acceptance. A minute or two later, he was opening the sliding door so that she could drag her kitbag inside – it wouldn't have done for him, an officer, to help her – and then, 'I say, I'll just pull down the blinds to the corridor ... I think it would be safer ...

the guard, you know.'

Numbly she nodded her agreement and sat down opposite him, her knees pressed so tightly together that he could see the whiteness of the bone through the delightfully sheer black stocking. Watson, he said to himself, remembering the Sherlock Holmes stories of his youth, the game's afoot...

It was.

Shortly before Peterborough, the long, slow troop train came to a sudden stop. The Germans were bombing the big city. They would have to remain in the countryside until the raid was over. Till then all lighting was to be extinguished and even the engine's boilers were to be dampened down in case the Dorniers droning overhead caught a glimpse of the stationary train. It was a situation that suited Fleming ideally: alone with the frightened young innocent in a darkened compartment – a bed on wheels, in fact. What could go wrong?

Nothing did.

The delight of it all, he breathed to himself, as he felt her shudder and stiffen when his hand rasped against the artificial silk of her black stockings. How her body tensed as those hot fingers penetrated even further! For a moment her right hand seemed as if it were about to push him away. But a hot kiss on her soft lips and she desisted...

159

It had almost been too easy. But he had forced himself to play according to the rules of the game, so that he extracted full enjoyment out of the actual deflowerment. How he loved that Victorian term with all its delightful degenerate connotations. *'I must ... please don't stop me now ... It won't hurt ... I'll be careful, I swear to you...'*

An hour later when the train to London finally got the 'all-clear' and could continue its snail-like pace to London, Fleming satiated now, with the girl snuggled warmly in his arms – he'd take her back to his flat for another session, once they reached the capital – he remembered Admiral Godfrey's words to him the week before when he had been looking into the case of the medium-spy, known as 'Madame Clarrisa'.

At the end of a confused meeting on the problem of the German high sea fleet, his chief had snorted in his usual quarterdeck fashion: 'There must be a connection.'

A slightly puzzled Fleming had retorted, 'A connection between what, sir?' But Admiral Godfrey, his face a brick-red colour, perhaps due to anger, had not replied, leaving Fleming more confused than ever.

Now as Fleming prepared to move, his right hand still resting almost protectively on the Wren's throbbing loins, he saw the connection at last – and the way ahead.

The Hun would make a big ploy to cover the exit to the Baltic. Their planes would be in full force, fighting off nosey Coastal Command reconnaissance planes. They'd lay new and uncharted minefields to prevent RN subs and coastal craft from penetrating the Baltic to spy on their surface ships. In essence, the Hun would attempt to seal off the inland sea until the time came for their ships to make their major sally into the North Sea and against the British Home Fleet, if that's what they were after.

That time would come when the weather conditions were favourable to them – fog, low cloud, heavy rain and the like which would conceal their dash through the Baltic narrows into the open sea beyond. But there'd be a catch. The longer the German fleet's progress through the Baltic to that exit, the more likely the listening stations in Scotland and the British legation's secret operations in Sweden would pick up their radio traffic indicating movement westwards. So?

As the train slowed down and outside in the steamy fug of the corridor, the exhausted troops started to put on their heavy equipment, praying that the good ladies of the WVS would be waiting for them on the platform with mugs of hot char. Fleming had it in a nutshell. Bomb the hell out of every port along the Baltic, east of Wilhelm-shaven, forcing the fleet ever deeper into the Baltic, perhaps as far as Danzig. Then when they did come out, it might well take them a day to reach the mouth of the inland sea, without any chance of returning to the shelter of one of the smaller ports – and in a day a damn lot of bloody nasty things could happen in wartime.

Fleming waited till the Wren had patted herself into shape, set her cap at a regulation navy angle and then helping her to put her heavy blue kitbag over her shoulder, he followed her down to the platform, admiring the pretty sway of her trim buttocks beneath the tight blue serge of her skirt. His staff car was waiting, as planned.

The rating behind the wheel looked at the two of them. Fleming's eyes narrowed threateningly. The rating saluted and held the door open. Fleming indicated that the Wren should sit in front next to the driver, while he took his seat in the rear – it wouldn't do for a lower rank to be seen sitting next to an officer when they arrived at the Admiralty. The Wren didn't mind, obviously. She was thrilled to be in a chauffeur-driven car for the first time in her young life. At her side, the driver, an old 'three-stripper', told himself that the boss had been up her navy blue bloomers this night, he'd be bound.

But Fleming had already forgotten the girl. His mind was too full of the scheme he would soon be proposing to Admiral Godfrey at 'White's'.

Savage's Statement

'I shook my head – and the next moment bloody well wished I hadn't. It felt as if a red-hot metal skewer had been bored into the back of my bloody skull. I shook my head and everything swung into focus. I wish it hadn't. There was horror upon horror everywhere I looked.

'The RAF raid had caught the port defences completely by surprise. Just as we'd gone aboard with the supplies, the medium bombers – Wellingtons, I think they were – had come out of the sun, right across the water, mast-hopping almost, and had begun the raid. Brave bastards for Brylcreem boys, you had to admit that. One false move and they would have been in the drink themselves. Besides they had to be pretty nifty with their bomb-dropping. At that low height, if they'd timed it wrong, they could have blown themselves to hell and back.

'Now all was fire, fury and mass confusion. There were dead Danes and German civvies all over the show. Elena, thank God, hadn't been hit. I grabbed her – she was pretty dazed – and yelled, "Let's get the hell out of here before they come back." She protested: a woman next to her in the rubble needed help. But when she grabbed the woman's arm, the poor bitch toppled over. The back of her head was missing. Elena's face turned to horror – and we ran for it.'

Listening to the stiff old man, I was amazed. There was a vital young man beneath that old-fashioned exterior propped up by the cushions of the Parker-Knoll.

'Somehow or other we got off the ship – there was no sign of the "Zhid" anywhere, but we weren't particularly concerned. Not only did we want to get away from the next flight of bombers, we also had to reckon with rescue parties. Once they came on the scene and started asking questions, who knows?'

I nodded, but said nothing.

'God, it was like the end of the world, though. You can hardly imagine the horrors. I even felt sorry for the Huns. A woman ran up to us, for instance, completely naked, her hair on fire, screaming for help ... another lay in the gutter, a dead baby clasped to her breast, still alive and writhing as the flames consumed her. I remember her whispering, "*Phosphor*". The RAF had dropped incendiaries with the bloody awful stuff in it, you see. And then she shrieked "Shoot me..."

But nobody had a pistol – or the time. Everywhere everyone was trying to escape just like we were ... Dante's *Inferno* and all that.'

Again, I nodded and said nothing. Savage's story was horrific. But he wanted to tell me everything. I can no longer recall the precise words he used to describe all that he saw...

He and the girl had experienced the worse of a phosphorus attack. There were folks who had been hit by the deadly white pellets, which had imbedded themselves in people's skin and had continued to burn as long as they were exposed to air.

When the flames continued to rise and rise, these hapless people had run in circles like rabid dogs: men, women and kids running crazily, screaming hysterically, stumbling and falling, knowing that only water could save them from being burned alive.

Revolted, the two fugitives watched impotently as a woman, already blind, her face steadily being eaten away by the flickering white flame, fell into the shallow water off the quay and drowned, the water stiffling her terrible screaming in the end.

They stumbled on, eyes shielded against the searing flame, trying to find a way out of this hell-hole, blundering blindly through the burning streets, as the great fire storm thundered to its orgiastic climax, the houses on both sides shuddering like stage back-drops with, at regular intervals, whole build-ings sliding down in an avalanche of bricks and stones.

'This is nothing to do with God,' an old man quavered from a doorway as they fought their way out of the inferno. 'It's the work of man...' He reached out one of his burned claws, like a charred twig, and tried to grab hold of Savage, pleading, 'Take me with you, friend ... please take me...'

Savage recoiled with horror and, when that monstrous claw clutched his singed jacket, he lashed out with all his strength and sent the old man reeling back into the burning ruins.

On and on the two of them went – blindly. They didn't know where they were going. All they knew was that they had to escape ... to escape from this crazy, doomed place. At his side, Elena cried, the tears streaming down her ashen face. Brutally, however, Savage dragged her with him, tears or not. She mustn't be allowed to break down now, he knew that implicitly. It would be fatal. She'd never start again. Who could under these conditions?

They passed a kindergarten. A collection of women and children lay in a neat line, fused together as they had stood, not a mark on them, their faces glowing a healthy red.

The fire storm had choked the very air out of their lungs and killed them as they had waited to enter the place.

I remember Savage's face when he recounted the dreadful story.

'That nearly did for me, I can tell you,' Savage said in a low voice, his mind obviously full of that terrible memory. 'If it hadn't been for Elena,' he hesitated momentarily, as if, even now, nearly sixty years later, the girl who vanished so long ago, could still tug at his heartstrings. 'I don't think I would have been able to proceed any further. I'd have found a corner and just let it happen – death.'

Looking at him now, even though the mark of death was already upon him, I didn't think Vice-Admiral Horatio Savage would ever have given in. It wasn't in the nature of the beast. But I didn't remark upon the fact.

Apparently, the lovers faced more horrors before it all finally ended: a team of horses, wild-eyed and panicked, their manes on fire, dragging a cart with a headless driver in the seat; naked babies from a shattered maternity home blown into skeletal trees, trapped in the blackened branches like monstrous human fruit; charred pygmies who had once been fully grown soldiers, their skin burst and oozing a purple juice like the syrup of overripe figs. Heat radiation sucking away

168

the lives of trapped victims, their eyes bulging and glistening indicating that they were still alive ... until the eyes themselves burst out of their skulls under that tremendous pressure and they were dead at last ... *Horror upon horror...*

It was, however, when they came to the trapped Canadian that their attempt to escape came to an end and their lives were changed irrevocably. He was hanging from a large tree by his torn parachute, his right arm limp and useless, as if it were broken, looking down at the angry mob surrounding the place. They were shouting, waving their fists, with children throwing the cobbles they had turfed up from the pavement. It didn't worry the Canadian in the blue of the RAF. He looked down, his face very pale as if he were in acute pain, and shouted back in defiance, 'You kids, can't you even frigging pitch a rock right ... Hey, one of you Krauts, don't look so dumb, get me down ... My goddam arm is broken.'

Shocked beyond all measure as they were, Savage could only admire the lone Canadian's bravery. His days were numbered. That was obvious. If the police didn't get here soon and save him, the mob might well lynch him. Savage knew it wouldn't be the first time that the victims of an RAF raid had taken their revenge on some unfortunate, downed crewman; it wouldn't be the last, either. German civilians, normally tolerant of POWs and the like, hated British terror fliers with a passion.

But there was another threat to the Canadian's life, which was approaching fast – the flaming inferno. Wafted by the wind from the sea, the flames were mounting higher and higher, jumping from street to street, rushing towards the Canadian suspended helplessly from the free. The trapped man was putting a brave face on it, but he knew that if the mob didn't pull him down and perhaps lynch him, the flames would get him. Perhaps that was why he called in broken German, no longer so defiant. *'Hilfe ... ich bin verletzt...'* and then in English pitifully, 'Come on ... give a guy a break, folks, I can't make it by myself...' He looked round wildly at the sea of angry faces. 'Shoot me if you like ... but hell, I'm gonna fry up here in a minute. *Hilfe leute.'*

Savage looked at Elena. She was still terrified, but there were tears of pity in her beautiful eyes and he knew instinctively what she wanted him to do, whatever the cost to them personally. He cleared his throat and raised his blood-stained hand. *'Hor zu,'* he commenced.

Here and there, members of the lynch mob turned and gazed at him, wondering why this man, who was clearly a foreigner, was addressing them. But the rest continued their threats, raising their fists to the trapped Canadian, as he recoiled, trying to make his body smaller as the flames grew ever closer.

Savage raised his voice. '*Hor zu,*' he repeated. 'Listen ... Don't—' He stopped short. At the edge of the crowd, a fat policeman, minus leather helmet, his tunic singed and smoking, had pulled out his pistol, his fat paw trembling wildly. The Canadian had already seen him, and ceased his wriggling, his attempts to escape the encroaching flames. It was as if he knew he was going to die and was going to do so like a man. For one long instant the whole scene froze as if for eternity: Savage, the Canadian about to die, the flaming city, the hate-filled mob. It was a picture that the world's greatest artist could never have painted, even if such a painter had been present. It was something beyond the ken of even a genius: a scene that could never be reproduced. But, for Savage, it would be seared on to his mind's eye till the day he died.

And then a dying plane came winging its way in, both engines afire, the crew staring – petrified – through their perspex portholes. Even before they realised it was there, it smashed into the street and in an instant as the Vice-Admiral now croaked, 'I knew it was the end. This time we were all going for a Burton.'

He sighed. 'When I look back now, it would have been better if we had done...' He sighed yet again. 'I would have been spared a lot of heartache.' And then he raised his voice and said, 'Nurse, bring the bowl. I think I'm going to be sick again.' And he was.

BOOK THREE

Into Battle

One

Winston Churchill rose from the huge Victorian bathtub like a toothless, pink Buddha. The water dripped from his pudgy arm as the valet rushed across the tight bedroom at Chequers to offer him his false teeth on a silver platter.

The Prime Minister thrust them between his gums and grinned at the embarrassed delegation from the Admiralty, which had been ushered into his bathroom. Surprisingly, the Great Man himself had called his bodyguard, Inspector Thompson, to say, 'Wheel 'em in, Inspector. They're sailors. They've seen plenty of naked rumps in their time, I'll be bound.' A statement which had made Admiral Lord Pound gasp. Fleming, behind his chief, Admiral Godfrey, had grinned. It was a remark he'd note for the future. Indeed he'd make a note of the whole scene: the 'King's First Minister', as Churchill liked to call himself in the fashion of the eighteenth century, receiving the brass hats of the Admiralty in bare buff. There was more

175

to come.

Churchill stood up and nodded again to the valet. The valet snapped into action at once. As if by magic, he produced a large cigar, which Churchill momentarily savoured under his nose before lighting it, a maliciously cheeky look in his clever eyes, as if he were watching the admirals' reactions. Fleming chuckled to himself. The Great Man was toying with them and was enjoying himself immensely as he did so.

Standing there completely naked, his plump hairless body dripping with water, he waited till a footman appeared, beaing a tray with drinks and glasses. 'Drinks, gentlemen?' he asked airily, as the footman waited for orders.

Admirals Pound and Frazier looked shocked. 'But sir,' Pound exclaimed, 'it's still only ten in the morning. I don't feel—'

Churchill cut him short, 'Never too early for a drink, Pound. Keeps a man healthy and flexible. There are too many sober-sided people about in this country, fighting the first war still.' He nodded to the footman. The latter poured him out a stiff peg of malt whisky, while the first one draped a fluffy white dressing gown around the Prime Minister's shoulders so that now instead of Buddha, he looked like an ancient polar bear which had seen much better days.

With Churchill in the lead, puffing at the big double Havana and carrying his large glass of whisky, they proceeded into the dressing-room, presided over by Churchill's sole bodyguard, the Scotland Yard inspector, and sat down the best they could on the spindly antique furniture.

Churchill took a careful sip of his whisky and Fleming noted that the Great Man did everything for effect. He wasn't really a hard-drinking, hard-smoking type. This show of anti-bourgeois behaviour was to put the admirals in their place; to make it clear to them that he didn't expect conventional wisdom and suggestions from them. He wanted dramatic, innovative policies and strategies. The young future writer, Fleming, realised that Churchill, ever since he had come to power in May of the previous year, had been battling against an entrenched establishment.

Now Churchill wasted no time. The show was over. He wanted business – and results. 'I've read your report, Fleming,' he snapped. 'You have done well by your chief. Well expressed and to the point. Good.'

Fleming actually blushed. Admiral Godfrey looked pleased – and relieved. He didn't want to bear the brunt of Churchill's rage – the Great Man definitely had no respect for people; admirals could be fired at the snap of a finger and thumb.

'So, gentlemen, where do we stand?' Churchill answered his own question. 'Here. The Hun wants to pull off some spectacular feat with his surface ships before the balloon goes up in Russia, when Hitler will have his hands full in that country.' Churchill saw the looks on their faces and swiftly added, 'Our special source of intelligence indicates that Mr Hitler will march east next month. So what can the Hun admirals do?'

'They'll attack one of our convoys and then make a run for it, back to the Baltic or north to Norway, perhaps south to their ports in occupied France – Lorient, Brest and the like,' Pound finally got a word in. 'They've done it before, after all.'

Churchill looked at the slab-faced senior admiral almost pityingly. 'It's a possibility, but a remote one. They might use one of our convoys as a *bait*. But would the Hun risk his great ships, such as the *Bismarck*, just to sink a few merchant men bringing corned beef from America to the suffering people of this land? I doubt it ... I doubt it strongly, gentlemen.'

Pound had been lectured long enough. In his no-nonsense manner – which in the past had made many a senior officer under his command quail – he snapped, 'Pray, then, sir, tell us what the Hun intends.'

178

Churchill ignored the heavy irony of the senior admiral's words. He knew that he had gotten a rise from Pound. So he smiled and answered, 'Of course, I will, my dear Pound. In the last bit of unpleasantness, the German Imperial High Sea Fleet was accused by its own people of sitting in its harbours on its iron-clad bum doing exactly nothing. Its reticence was supposedly based on false strategic assumptions. The result was the mutiny of the High Sea Fleet in 1918. Now, however, there is a new kind of strategic thinking aboard Mr Hitler's Navy.'

Fleming wondered how Churchill could know all this, but he listened intently all the same. The Prime Minister's discourse was fascinating.

'That is, "Don't let us be too careful this time".' Churchill shot a cocky sideways glance at his admirals, as if he were indirectly advising them not to fall into the same trap themselves. 'The result?' Again Churchill answered his own rhetorical question. 'The Huns are prepared for bold action – and, mark this, *losses*!' He paused to let his words sink in. 'This time they'll go for our battleships, even if we do outnumber them, and risk all. In short, gentlemen, an attack by their great ships on our convoys will only be a ploy to lure our battleships to the scene for an all-out battle.' He paused, and took a careful sip of his drink, a pensive expression on his face.

Now Fleming could see that the bantering, mocking attitude had vanished. The Great Man was serious. Fleming knew why. The British capital ships, with the exception of the *Prince of Wales*, which was still undergoing trials with scores of civvies still on board, were hopelessly outmoded in comparison with the Germans'. Even HMS *Hood*, Britain's largest and fastest ship, had been built in 1918. The *Bismarck*, on the other hand, had been laid down only a couple of years ago. If the Germans got loose, and attracted only part of the British Home Fleet, located far north at Scapa Flow, the enemy might well wipe the floor with the outdated, outgunned British ships. After all, back in 1939, it had taken five or six British cruisers to sink the modern German *Graf Spee*.

'So, gentlemen, what can we do?' Churchill was deadly serious now. The mocking look in his eyes had given way to one of determination and defiance, that same look which had seen Britain through Dunkirk and the Battle of Britain the year before. 'We must be on the alert to mass our forces immediately once the *Bismarck* and her attendant ships make a break from the Baltic. As the Hun says, '*Klotzen* ... er.' He cursed under his breath. Obviously he had forgotten the rest of the German military term.

'*Nicht Kleckern*,' a happy Fleming supplied the rest of the phrase.

Godfrey smiled at the cleverness of his aide. The two senior admirals frowned at such temerity from a junior member of the Wavy Navy.

'That's it,' Churchill said. 'Concentrate not dissipate. We must outnumber the *Bismarck*. We have to have that superiority in numbers, gentlemen, or there will be a tragedy that the Royal Navy will never live down...'

Sombrely, the naval party walked back down the gravel path to their waiting staff cars. They did so in silence, each man wrapped up in a cocoon of his own thoughts. The Great Man's words and his final warning had had their intended effect. Even Fleming felt subdued, his own private ambitions forgotten for a while as a result of what Churchill had said.

'There will be a tragedy that the Royal Navy will never live down.' All the way back to London, Churchill's dramatic warning echoed through the caverns of Fleming's mind, and even the prospect of further perverting the willing little Wren that night could not divert his brain from Churchill's final statement, until Admiral Godfrey, sitting next to him at the back of the staff car, roused himself from his doze to say, 'Old Winnie does go on a bit, Ian ... But then I suppose all those frocks' – he meant politicians – 'are like that, what?'

Dutifully Fleming agreed with his chief. But for once he knew this was not just the spoutings of a 'frock'. Churchill really meant it ... A *tragedy* ... But how?

Five hundred miles or so away that same morning, as the Wavy Navy party crept into a shabby war-torn London, with the barrage balloons tethered above Whitehall like lead-coloured elephants, Admiral Raeder and his staff were working out the details of *that* tragedy to come.

Now, time was of the essence. The Führer, ready to march on Russia, was breathing down Raeder's neck. He was to give the German people a victory and then, as far as the landlubber, Hitler – who was seasick even in harbour – was concerned, the German Surface Fleet had played its role in the West for good. But Raeder, as pedantic and thorough as ever, knew he had to cut corners now. There was no time to perfect things, even though he was risking his great ships, especially the pride of the *Kriegsmarine*, the *Bismarck*.

Despite the protest of his older staff officers, who thought like he did, he was sending his ships to battle without their full complements of fuel, ammunition, and even crew. 'There is no time,' was his standard retort, when one of his officers complained. *'Tempo ... Tempo ... Der Führer will es so. Klar?'* And, as always, there was no way that anyone could get round the Führer's edict.

Still, as Raeder looked out on the crowded docks below, from Danzig's Naval HQ, he felt a huge sense of pride – he was staring directly at the great ship, the *Bismarck*. Even as she was, only half prepared for battle, not even 'worked up' properly – for they had had to cut its maritime trials short to meet the Führer's demands – she was an imposing, beautiful ship.

The *Bismarck* was the strongest battleship in the world. She displaced 50,000 tons, and forty per cent of that great weight was armour, best Krupp steel, of the kind that the Englishmen's older ships simply could not match. Yet despite this enormous weight of protective armour, she had a speed of twenty-nine knots and the British Navy only had one ship capable of catching her at that speed. It was the English battle cruiser, HMS *Hood*, which had a top speed of thirty-two knots.

Admittedly, the *Hood* had an impressive speed and could fire an awesome volume of shot and shell. But she had the fatal weakness of being a battle cruiser. Armour had been sacrificed for speed and Raeder, watching and brooding, knew exactly what her secret weakness was and what armour had been added to the Tommy ship since she had been launched back in 1918.

One week after Hitler and Raeder had finalised the operation the first piece of really bad news came in from France. It was conveyed by no less a person than Rear Admiral Karl Doenitz, head of the U-Boat Army. He had flown straight to Danzig from Brest where he had been inspecting U-Boat wolf packs. Passing on this top secret information to the older admiral gave him the greatest of pleasure.

Without any ceremony, he was taken straight from the little airfield to the office where Raeder and a stern-faced Admiral Lutjens, commander of the *Bismarck*, were anxiously waiting for him. Doenitz commenced without preliminaries, his hard, lean, ruthless face concealing his delight at the bad news he had brought from occupied France.

'Both the *Gneisnau* and *Scharnhorst* will not be ready for sea in time, Herr Grossadmiral,' he announced baldly. 'I have it from the Rear Admiral Engineering, who is personally in charge of the French yards.'

With a shaky hand Raeder felt for his old-fashioned starched wing-collar, as if it were suddenly unbearably tight. 'Won't be—'

'Yes sir. The damage they suffered is too extensive for an emergency.' Doenitz took his gaze from the stricken elderly admiral and looked at Lutjens. 'You won't have the escort of the two battle cruisers now, of course.'

Lutjens was of a different mould than the Grand Admiral. He snapped in his harsh north German accent, glaring at Doenitz, as if he would have liked to have strangled his scraggy neck there and then, 'Of course.' Then ignoring a triumphant Doenitz, he said to the stricken Raeder, 'Sir, this means we must postpone or cancel the operation.'

Raeder looked at him weakly. 'Cancel ... postpone?' he echoed.

'Yes sir. It stands to reason. All we've got in the way of an additional capital ship to support the *Bismarck* is the *Prinz Eugen* – and she's been damaged too. To make a success of this operation we need the strength and firepower of the two battle cruisers, *Scharnhorst* and *Gneisnau*. Now, according to Doenitz here,' he didn't even deign to look at the U-boat commander, 'we haven't got them. The op is now too risky. A decision will have to be made.'

Raeder opened his mouth like a fish out of water. It seemed to take him an age to find his voice, while Doenitz watched, his contempt and delight barely concealed. Finally he managed to say. 'We have to go ahead. You know why, Lutjens. If we postpone this operation for now and even if the Führer were to approve of it, which I doubt, it will be summer before we can start again. Who knows then, if we will be putting to sea at all.'

Lutjens opened his mouth, as if to protest again. Then he thought better of it; he knew there was no hope.

'There is no other choice, Lutjens,' he heard Raeder say in a faint toneless voice, as if he were speaking to himself really and had already forgotten the presence of the other two admirals. 'The *Bismarck* and the *Prinz Eugen* must put out alone ... come what may.'

The decision had been made.

Two

Savage groaned.

Slowly, tentatively he opened his right eye. He groaned even more. He wished he hadn't moved. It felt as if a red-hot poker was skewering its way into the bruised eye from the back of his bloody head. They really had worked him over the night before.

He would have liked to have drifted back into unconsciousness, but his sense of anger – and duty – would not allow him to do so. He had to work out what had happened to him since the air raid and what exactly his situation was now.

He forced both eyes open. The red mist drifted away and things started to come into focus. He was in a cell, blurred by his defective vision, but a prison cell without doubt. He attempted to sit up and realised the very next instant, his eyes were misleading him. His right foot was chained to the floor next to the cement slab which served as a bed. 'Blast and damn,' he cursed and closed his eyes momentarily. He visualised the scene after they had been pulled from the smoking rubble: he remembered those harsh words that rang with an air of finality, *'Geheime Staatspolizei – sie sind verhaftet ... Kommen Sie mit.'* He realised he was in a real mess.

Twice, the fat civilian from the Gestapo had beaten him up. It had been a routine beating. The Gestapo man, with the stump of a cheap unlit cigar clenched between his thick lips, had struck him time and time again with his brass knuckles and, when Savage had threatened to lose consciousness, he had dragged him to the cheap pail full of dirty water in the corner of the interrogation room and thrust his head into it until he had come up spluttering and choking for breath, but again ready for the next beating.

But at the end of it all, the torturer had been quite content with the information he could have easily got from Savage's POW camp records: name, rank and age. He had not even asked about Elena.

Now slumped there on the concrete slab, with the spring sunshine peering fitfully through the iron bars of the cell aperture, an alarming thought shot through Savage's aching head: *what had happened to the beautiful Polish girl, who had risked all in coming with him?*

But before he had time to set his poor

188

addled brain to work on that mystery, a harsh shout came echoing down the long corridor outside. *'Achtung!'* But this was not the command Savage had heard often enough in Wesertimke POW camp. *'ACHT – TUNG.'* It was the cry given only when some outstanding, feared personage was about to make his appearance.

Even in his weakened, battered state, Savage forced himself, with a rattle of chains, to sit upright on the stone bunk and run his dirty hand through his rumpled, blood-matted hair.

Just in time. There was an officious rattle of keys. His door swung open with a rusty squeak. His tormentor of the previous night hurried across the cell. Now his evil eyes showed nothing, but a sense of urgent duty and obedience, as if he dare not give any hint of his real personality – in case. Hastily he undid the chain and hissed in Savage's ear. *'Aufstehen, Mensch ... aufstehen ... los, dalli AUFSTEHEN.'*

When Savage hesitated, the Gestapo man dragged him to his feet and held him there, swaying badly until the blood returned to his legs and he could stand unaided. Just in the time. In that same moment, Savage heard the self-important stamp of boots in the corridor. The Gestapo man stamped to attention and his right arm shot out rigidly. 'Heil

Hitler,' he barked at the top of his voice, as the small party swung into the cell, blundering against each other as they did so, as if they were not prepared to give way to one another because it was a matter of protocol and prestige.

Under other circumstances Savage might have laughed at these fat, arrogant Germans in their fancy uniforms, laden with braid and cheap tin decorations, each carrying a revolver in a holster at his belt, as if he half expected to be fighting for his life at the very next moment.

But there was nothing faintly comical about the little man standing in their midst, dwarfed by the heavy-set, over-fed Gestapo thugs. Even though he didn't know it at the time, Savage guessed this was the boss. Those cold dark eyes and shaven skull made that perfectly clear. Vaguely, the boss, if that was what he was, returned the salute and commanded not too loud, as if he expected people to strain if they wished to hear his words, '*Wegtreten! ... Bitte.*'

Immediately, the entourage turned as one and once more pushed and shoved each other in their attempt to leave through the narrow open door of the cell, while the little man waited, his heavy dark face revealing nothing. Finally he nodded to the man at the entrance, '*Scharführer.*'

The latter responded immediately. '*Sonder-führer*!' he yelled, while Savage watched the various movements, only half understanding what was going on, but feeling as if he were watching the 'Crazy Gang' at some Palladium knock-about farce, performing their crazy antics to illogical rules known only to themselves.

As the footsteps approached, the little man turned back to Savage. '*Gestatten, Standartenführer Müller,*' he snapped, clicking his heels together noisily. '*Sie sprechen Deutsch?*'

Savage shrugged slightly. '*Ein wenig,*' he replied.

The little man named Müller rattled off a great burst of German, looking intently at the prisoner with those dark frightening eyes of his.

Savage looked up at him. '*Nix verstehen,*' he said helplessly, wondering why they had wheeled in such an obvious Gestapo bigshot to question him – just an ordinary 'kriegie', who had had the misfortune to be caught red-handed. Then the thought flashed through his numb, befuddled brain with alarming speed, was it because of Elena? Did the fact that he was being aided by a Polish slave worker, a Slavic sub-human, warrant special attention? But before he had time to put his fears into hesitant German, Gestapo Müller (for it was he) shouted as if he were

191

on some huge barrack square, '*Sonderführer?*'
Savage knew what a '*sonderführer*' was.
They had had them in the camp: a kind of
civilian with special skills, who dressed in a
uniform like a soldier, but wasn't really part
of the Army. This meant they had rights and
privileges not accorded to someone who
came under Army rules and regulations. But
Savage had never seen a *sonderführer* like
this.

It was the *zhid*, as Elena had called him.
The fat communist Jew with the cunning
dark eyes, who had played the *Internationale*
so openly in the waterfront bar and had
promised to help them escape to Sweden
before the bombing. Now he was tucked
carelessly into an ill-fitting brown uniform,
with a swastika armband, and an oversized
peaked cap gracing his head, an unholy grin
on his broad face, as if he were enjoying the
look of total, absolute surprise on the
prisoner's face.

He bowed politely as he entered the cell
and said, 'Good morning, Mr Savage. I hope
you are feeling better.' His look of happiness
increased as he saw that the prisoner was
now even more surprised by the fact that he
knew his name.

But Gestapo Müller had no time for such
pleasantries, especially when he didn't
understand them. 'Close the door, *Sonder-*

192

führer,' he said sharply. 'This damned place is full of big ears.'

The *Sonderführer*'s smile vanished. He closed the door hastily and then listened intently, as the Gestapo boss fired a series of questions at Savage,

'All right,' the fat Jew said finally, 'this gentleman has a few questions to ask you. I shall translate. But I shall warn you now, this is what will happen if you speak one word of what is said here.' He drew his right forefinger dramatically beneath his throat jowls, as if he were slitting a throat.

Savage was not impressed. Indeed his bewilderment had now been replaced by a burning anger. He snorted, 'Where is the Polish girl ... Eh, come on, out with it, or I'll tear you apart with my bare hands!'

The naked aggression in Savage's face must have scared the *Sonderführer*. For although Savage was tethered to the stone bed, he stepped back a pace or two, as if he feared for his life. Müller snapped, '*Los, mach' weiter, Arsch mit Ohren.*'

The 'arse with ears' recovered quickly and answered, 'The Polack woman will be all right, as long as you behave yourself, Savage. Now let's get on with it.' He paused. Müller nodded. He took a deep breath like a diver about to jump from the high board. 'How would you like to go to Sweden, *as a free man?*' he asked after a moment's deliberation. 'From there your own people at the legation will ensure that you are sent straight home without being interned by the Swedes, as is usually the case.' He paused and looked straight at an obviously puzzled Savage.

Savage was indeed puzzled. Everything was happening fast, even the *Sonderführer*'s English had improved dramatically since he had met him as a supposedly seedy Communist in the sailors' waterfront hang out. Dimly, Savage was aware that he had been caught up in some sort of mysterious plot in which he was just a mere cog in the wheel. But what was that plot and why had this – er – Gestapo Müller gone to such great lengths to entrap him, a humble escaped POW and junior officer in the Navy? What the hell was going on?

The *Sonderführer* seemed to be able to read the prisoner's mind for he added easily, 'Rest assured that you will be doing nothing to harm your own country. On the contrary, you will be aiding it.'

'Aiding it? But,' he pointed to the shaven-headed chief of the Gestapo, standing there, arms folded impatiently, as if he couldn't get this business over with quickly enough. 'But,' he repeated... 'Him?' He didn't seem able to clarify his thoughts any further.

'We're in this together, Savage. Now what

is it to be? Are you with us? You scratch us and we'll scratch you, as I believe the English say.' He smiled winningly. 'What is it going to be?'

'The girl?'

'She'll remain here till the business is over. But you have our word on it, nothing will happen to her. Besides,' the *Sonderführer*'s smile vanished as abruptly as it had come, 'you have nothing to lose and everything to gain.' He turned and hastily whispered something to Müller.

The latter nodded his shaven head urgently.

'If you don't agree, you die,' the *Sonderführer* said. 'You already know too much. So what are you going to do?'

Savage gave in. 'As long as the girl is OK—' He didn't finish his sentence. The two of them, the fat Jew and the hard-faced Gestapo boss, were not listening, he realised. They were too eager to talk themselves. He waited...

Three

A high silver moon hung over the drifting wisps of night fog. It cast a spectral light on the grey sea of the channel. A wind was beginning to spring up. But as yet it was not strong enough to sweep away the vestiges of the fog. It looked as if the predictions of the weathermen would be right. Patchy, low-level fog would remain with them till mid-morning at least.

It was a forecast which made the officers on the bridge of the *Bismarck* happy. It made for difficult navigation. All the same the fog would give them the cover they needed as they slipped out of Danzig. By the time the high-level Tommy reconnaissance planes attempted to breach the port's defences and take photographs, they'd be gone and out into the Baltic.

Now, followed by the smaller, less powerful *Prinz Eugen*, the *Bismarck* ploughed steadily through the cold grey swell, the tugs falling behind into the gloom. The only sound that could be heard was deep, throbbing one –

the notes of the great ship's powerful diesels and the steady pace of the many sentries. For Lutjens had ordered double look-outs and sentries for the great break out. One couldn't be too careful. Now they had a run of some twenty hours through the inland sea and that could be very dangerous, especially with the neutral Swedes – so important for the German war economy – sailing everywhere.

Lutjens, standing on the bridge, smoked silently and reflectively. Well, he told himself, if any damned fat Swede got in the way and attempted to earn a few kroner by reporting the *Bismarck*'s presence in the Baltic, he was going to be in for an unpleasant surprise. He'd be at the bottom of the sea before he knew what had hit him.

Lutjens smiled wryly at the thought of some well-rounded Swedish skipper being confronted by the realities of this global, total war. That'd surprise the bastard, he concluded.

The Admiral dismissed the Swedes and, with his cigar cupped in the palm of his hand so that the red glow was not visible, he considered what it would be like. Action, as far as he was concerned, had been limited so far. Indeed the only time that a German surface ship had made a name for itself had been back in 1939 when Captain Hans

Langsdorff's *Graf Spee* had captured the world's headlines.

Langsdorff had destroyed fifty thousand tons of British shipping in a month without the loss of a single German life. He had become a hero, decorated by radio by the Führer himself. That December von Langsdorff must have felt on top of the world, the Admiral told himself, as he pondered the fate of his predecessor. He would have believed that no ship in the South Atlantic could stop him and his beloved *Graf Spee*. Yet within a matter of days, his whole proud reputation had been shattered by a collection of inferior Tommy light cruisers. He had been trapped and, although he had volunteered to fight it out to the end, the Führer, not trusting von Langsdorff to do so, had ordered him to scuttle his proud ship. He had done so and thereafter had obviously felt there was no other way out but suicide. What a fate for such an able and brave officer!

Lutjens tapped the end of his cheap working-man's cigar and wondered what *his* fate would be if things went wrong. The Führer had no feeling for the sea and those who sailed it. As for Raeder, well, he was basically concerned with his own career and future; he would do nothing to help the *Bismarck* if she got into trouble.

'*Wie gekommen, so zerronnen,*' Lutjens whispered to himself, as he stared at the spectral sea, as if he sought to find something there, and thought of those far-off days and the high hopes which had been shattered so brutally. He realised once again that there was nothing certain in this life, save death.

'Radar, sir.'

Lutjens turned, startled, shocked out of his reverie. He swung round. It was the assistant gunner controller, standing there like a frightened mid-shipman. 'What is it, Guns?'

'Fishing vessels, right on our course.'

'Ours?' he barked.

'No, sir. Swedes.' The young assistant gunner controller answered with a note of trepidation in his voice, as if he expected an outburst on the Admiral's part.

It failed to come. For Lutjens had realised that this was the first of the imponderables that he was going to be face on this cruise to an unknown battle. An instant decision was called for. 'How many?'

'Four, sir.'

'Heaven, arse and cloudburst,' the Admiral cursed. 'All right.' He made his decision, realising as he did so how calmly he could decide that in an hour or so a score or so of honest Swedish fishermen were going to die suddenly and savagely. 'Liquidate them.'

Hearing this harsh command, the gunnery officer paled a little underneath the weathered surface of his young face, but he recovered soon enough. Promptly, he touched a hand to his cap and snapped, '*Jawohl, Herr Admiral!*'

He turned and went, leaving Lutjens to stare at the sea, alone with his thoughts once more. They weren't good ones. His decision had not pleased him, but it had to be done, he told himself. You couldn't fight a war without hard decisions.

For a moment the newsreel of the *Graf Spee* at Montevideo Harbour flashed before him: the bubbles of trapped air exploding on the surface, the mops and brushes floating foolishly on the surface, following a model of the ship that some rating had probably made in his spare time to take home to his mother as a souvenir of the *Graf Spee*, now mocking the great vessel which had been its subject; and a seaman's cap trailing its black ribbons behind it. Would this be the fate of *Bismarck*, too?

'Arse with ears,' the Admiral cursed once again. 'Great crap on the Christmas tree, what do you think this is, Lutjens, a seminary for well-born ladies of a sensitive nature! This is shitting war. Now get on with it, damn you, man!'

He shivered. He had burned away the rage

with that crude outburst of seaman's language. Now he was the capable, cool commander once more. His fears had vanished too. On the contrary, he was filled with sudden energy and anticipation at the thought of wiping out the humiliation to the German Navy that it had suffered with the scuttling of the *Graf Spee*.

Lutjens pulled the collar of his naval greatcoat closer to his neck. It was growing colder. The fog had almost lifted now. The soft swell was bathed in a hard icy silver by the moon. It bathed the superstructure of the great vessel in its light too. It gave the *Bismarck* a shimmering, unearthly wraithlike appearance.

'A ghost ship, Admiral,' the voices at the back of his cropped head whispered. 'A ghost ship out for vengeance.'

The voices didn't disturb the Admiral. He nodded as if he approved of them, was used to them; as if they were part and parcel of his being. 'Are you satisfied now?'

This time Lutjens didn't acknowledge those strange spectral voices. Instead he stood there a moment longer, feeling the immense power beneath his feet, listening to the rhythm of the mighty engines, drinking it all in avidly ... absorbing the power and strength of *his* mighty ship. Before him the channel widened, as if it were inviting him to increase his speed, hurry to his date with destiny and what lay beyond...

The Junkers 88 night fighter had taken off ten minutes earlier from Jever Field in Schleswig-Holstein. Now, although it was still a little foggy, the pilot was managing very well with the aid of his radar and the light cast by the moon. He touched his throat-mike and called to the gunner midships. 'Keep your eyes peeled, Horst. It shouldn't be long now.'

'Like a tin of peeled tomatoes,' Horst replied cheekily.

Next to him, the co-pilot pressed his throat-mike and said to the pilot, 'Skipper, do we really attack without warning?'

The pilot nodded, not taking his eyes off his panel of green-glowing instruments for an instant. 'Yes – and there are to be no survivors, either.' He gave a little shrug. 'Total war and all that, you know, Kai.'

'But if we're caught. They are after all neutrals—'

The pilot, the only party member in the Junkers crew took his eyes off the instruments for a moment, and pulling rank, snapped, 'Listen Kai, I don't give a shit if they're Mongolians. We Germans will win this war, if we're hard enough, so there'll be no comebacks. One day soon, we'll be masters of

Europe and that's that. I'll have no more of that kind of defeatist chat, understood, Kai.'

'Understood, skipper,' the co-pilot said a little miserably and, at the same instant, the mid-ships gunner sang out excitedly, 'Got 'em in my glassy orbits, skipper. To port. In that break in the fog.'

The pilot didn't hesitate. 'Prepare for attack,' he cried.

He tilted the nose down. The Junkers seemed to fall out of the silver sky. Suddenly there they were, a little cluster of boats, nets out, lanterns outlining their shapes in a stark black. It was a perfect target.

Eyes glued on the boats which were getting larger and larger by the instant, the pilot cried over the intercom, 'Bomb aimer.'

He didn't need to say more.

The bomb aimer, lying flat on his stomach over the glass and perspex observation, yelled back. 'Bomb doors open ... Taking over now, skipper.'

'You're in charge,' the pilot yelled back, eyes behind the flying goggles bulging with the pressure. Next to him the co-pilot felt that old mixture of fear and exhilaration, as the bomb aimer took over control of the Junkers, which was hurtling towards the sea as if intent on smashing itself there.

'Steady ... steady now,' the aimer yelled, '*yes*, hold that course, skipper, will you?'

'Holding course!'

At nearly five hundred kilometres an hour, the Junkers headed straight for the boats. Next to him, thrust back against his seat by the tremendous centrifugal force, the co-pilot could have sworn he saw the startled white faces of the crew members staring up at this black angel of death, which had appeared so startlingly from nowhere.

'Now!' the bomb aimer yelled in a voice that the others could hardly recognise: it was thick and passionate, almost sexual. *'Bombs away!'*

'Holy shitting strawsack!' the co-pilot screamed, realising that the bomb aimer had released the bombs too soon; they were going to be the victims of their own weapon. *'BREAK ... BREAK...'* Too late. Below, the first of the stick exploded, right on target.

A great gout of red flame shot upwards. The leading boats were blasted by an enormous blow torch, which seared their length and set their timbers afire in the very same moment that they disintegrated. But the Junkers was hit too. Suddenly, it rose high into the air at an incredible speed, as if punched by a gigantic fist.

Frantically, eyes bulging like those of demented man, the pilot wrestled to control the stricken night fighter. To no avail! The Junkers shimmied and slithered all over the night sky, while below yet another salvo exploded, drowning the screams of the bomb aimer, who had been ripped from pubis to throat by a razor-sharp fragment of bomb, his guts flowing from the scarlet wound like a steaming snake.

But no one had time for the dying man's shrill screams of absolute agony. Now the survivors were battling to save the plane before it was too late. Both the pilot and his co-pilot worked at the controls, trying to force the shattered nose upwards, while white hot glycol spurted from the portside engine and splattered all over the shattered cockpit canopy.

But they were out of luck. Mid-ship, the terrified air gunner baled out. They saw him, parachute half opened, as he sailed by them. He slammed directly into the starboard engine. The blades sliced his head off neatly. Complete with flying helmet, it flew apart from the headless torso gushing thick dark-red blood. It disappeared into the glowing darkness like a child's football, abandoned by some careless kid.

The co-pilot gave up. Not the pilot. '*Himmel, Arsch und Zugenaht*,' he cursed, his face hollowed out to a ruddy death's head by the light of the greedy little flames which were beginning to lick the length of the crippled plane's fuselage. With all his strength, muscles bulging through his thin coverall, he fought the controls. 'Come on, you bastard ... come on ... stay up will you!' Next to him, the co-pilot buried his face in his hands and began to sob like some broken-hearted woman.

Fighting to the very last, though in his heart of hearts, the pilot knew it was hopeless, the shattered Junkers flew on. Behind, it left the sinking Swedish craft, as it skimmed the surface of the sea, virtually wave-hopping now, until finally disappearing altogether.

Four

Sven was already half drunk, though the sun had not yet peeped over the massed green ranks of the firs which almost ran down to the edge of the water. He had been there since before dawn. But, as yet, he had not had a single bite, and he was desperate. If he didn't catch enough fish to pay for his next ration of schnapps before the Swedish state liquor store closed promptly at noon, he would be sentenced to another long night without a drink. The thought tormented him. In the forest he could always trap enough game and soon the mushrooms would be reappearing, another part of his staple and free diet. But schnapps. That didn't grow wild and if he was caught manufacturing his own illegal alcohol from potatoes and currants, the cops would shove him behind bars for years; and then there'd be no booze at all. Christ Almighty, he had to catch some fish soon, or he wouldn't survive the rest of the day! He had long forgotten how to pray. As soon as he been freed from the stern dictates of the Lutheran church at the age of fourteen, he had forgotten his prayers immediately. Now, however, he folded his dirty calloused hands and, looking up at the morning sky, said, 'Please God, let me catch some sea trout. They bring more money on the market. Please God...'

But on that May morning, God was perhaps looking the other way, for after another half-hour of fruitless casting and trawling, Sven took a tiny, careful sip of his rationed schnapps and gave up. He'd tried. It was now that, for once in his life, Sven Hansen struck lucky.

Wandering along the lonely remote beach in a half-drunken daze he spotted the severed head first. It didn't startle him – he was too far gone for that. Then he saw the body a little further on, with the heap of what he supposed for a while was scrap metal, but which later on the *Polis* identified as the cockpit of a German Junkers 88.

Sven's mind worked with the deliberate slowness of the chronic alcoholic. All the same, he was sober enough to realise that there might be something of value in the strange heap of still-smoking metal that he could turn into schnapps. There was.

Two hours later Sven was roaring drunk on the proceeds of that surprising find and the local representative of the *Svenska Tageblatt* was urgently calling his Stockholm head office and a little later an unregistered telephone number not far away, crying excitedly over the poor line, 'Here they've found a Junkers. A drunk. No, you can't talk to him. He's blindo. Found some Nazi Iron Crosses ... flogged them for schnapps. But a Junkers all right ... Might be connected to the missing fishing boats ... I repeat, might be connected to the missing fishing boats...'

The news of the missing Swedish fishing boats in the Baltic and the remains of the crashed German night-fighters transmitted to the HQ of the British SIS in Stockholm, courtesy of the paid local reporter, struck home like a bombshell. The radio masts at the top of the embassy crackled. Teleprinters clattered furiously. Telephones and secure lines burned with the startling information, which all boiled down to that one overwhelming question: *is the* Bismarck *coming out...*?

Fleming had been aroused at his flat in the middle of the morning. The little naked Wren was still drunk from the champagne he had poured into her the night before and, as she had snuggled up to him cosily, he had tried to initiate her into the next stage of her 'trip down the slippery slope', as he had called it to himself.

'Sometimes, Peggy,' he had whispered,

softly stroking her tousled hair, 'a man is not always ready for – er – you know what.'

She had nodded dreamily, not opening her eyes, indulging herself in her fantasy that the handsome young officer really loved her.

'Then only the most drastic measures will work so that a man can show his loved one that he really cares for her. But she will have to help, of course.' He had pressed her plump young buttock gently.

'How?' she asked, still preoccupied with her silly girlish fantasies, with no idea of just how lecherous her companion was: a man who had seduced women ruthlessly and without remorse ever since he had been a schoolboy at Eton. Slowly, she opened one eye and looked up at him.

He had looked at her, as if he were burning with an unbearable love that would only end when death parted them. It was a look that he had practised many times in front of a mirror as a schoolboy. 'Should I show you?' he asked and tenderly planted a gentle kiss on her smooth innocent forehead.

'Of course,' she had responded, rising to the bait like an obedient trout, which she was, of course, he thought. 'Anything for you, darling.'

'Thank you, Peggy. You're a real sport. And remember, darling, I'd do the same for you any time.'

'I know, Ian,' she breathed, as he gently took hold of her head and brought it down to his chest.

She kissed it. Perhaps that, she thought, was what he expected her to do, the little romantic fool.

Emboldened, he forced her head a little further down his lean, pale-white body. He felt her stiffen. But it was only due to bewilderment. She was naturally wondering what she was supposed to do now. 'Oh, how good you are to me, Peggy,' he whispered with faked fervour. 'Oh, you know how to please a man.'

'Anything for you,' she began in a muffled voice in the same moment that he pushed her down to his hairy throbbing loins and she gave what he could only categorise as a squeak.

'You all right?' he queried in an anxious, caring voice, which was becoming husky now with sexual tension. 'Is this too much for you, dearest?' He felt himself sickened by the sound of his own voice, putting on this stupid bourgeois act for the girl's sake. But it had to be done. She had the makings of a good whore in her, he knew that now. Soon, with a bit more training and plenty of alcohol of course, he'd have her wild with frenzied excitement, ready to do just anything he wanted.

'Yes,' she murmured uncertainly, her mouth almost touching the still-dormant sexual organ, though he knew he wouldn't be able to control himself much longer: the intrinsic depravity of spoiling innocence was the best 'Spanish fly' in the world. 'But I don't...'

He bent and kissed the top of her head with fake tenderness. 'Just ... just take it in your mouth ... Only for a moment,' he added hastily. 'As a sign that you love me.'

'But isn't it ... dirty?' she asked plaintively. 'I mean—'

He kissed her again. 'Just a single moment,' he pleaded, feeling the movement, losing control over his loins. 'For me, Peggy, darling.'

She hesitated. Then he felt her fingers on him, guiding the erection in the direction of her tiny pink mouth, open already to expose the tongue, which he knew he could train to be as cunning as any Parisian whore's.

It was then that the telephone started to ring with startling suddenness and a moment later Admiral Godfrey was booming ever the air waves, as if he were still on the quarterdeck of the cruiser he had once commanded, 'Get over here, tootsweet, Ian ... The balloon's gone up at last...'

In Room 39, the headquarters of Admiral

Godfrey's Naval Intelligence, the balloon had, indeed, gone up. Just as in Stockholm, all was hectic activity. Phones rang without cease. Messengers hurried back and forth, Dispatch riders, laden with leather message pouches and sometimes carrying .38 revolvers in gloved hands came and went, speeding off to various military bases with new orders and instructions. Elegant aides and naval staff officers, all bouncing lanyards and handkerchiefs doused in expensive eau-de-Cologne, came hurrying in, demanding new information for their chiefs – '*bloody PDQ.*'

And all the while, Godfrey's clever young men, including Ian Fleming, tried every angle possible to break through the German barrier of silence about the Baltic. For a while Fleming, with his talent at female seduction, was luckier than the others. Some time back, for an emergency such as this one, he had gotten drunk and had seduced one of the ugliest of the key secretaries at the neutral US embassy in London.

The woman, all buck-teeth, plaintive mid-Western accent and 'long passion-freezers', as Fleming was wont to describe his conquest's underwear to his fellow officers, was madly in love with the aristocratic British officer. Twice she had betrayed key secrets relating to the ambassador, the Anglophobe, corrupt Joseph Kennedy, and had contributed in having him recalled to the States with his sons Jack and John. Now she was equally prepared to reveal what the US Berlin Embassy was sending back to London and Washington about the situation in the Baltic.

'Give me a drink, for God's sake,' Fleming had gasped melodramatically to his laughing fellow officers after a 'quickie' with her that midday in the back of a staff car. 'The things I do for bloody England and the Empire.' He had shuddered frighteningly. All the same he had brought back information which contributed greatly to the intelligence men's growing realisation that this was not another German feint, but the real thing.

'She said,' Fleming whispered between sips of the single malt that Admiral Godfrey produced himself, while the others clustered around him, eagerly waiting for his findings, 'that their Berlin Embassy press people have been put on alert for a key announcement from the *Tirpitzufer*.' He meant the German Admiralty in Berlin. 'They – the Yanks – have been warned to clear their lines to Washington. You know what that means? The Huns want President Roosevelt to be one of the first to know whatever they've got planned. If Roosevelt backs off and no longer supports Churchill, we've had it, chums.' Fleming suddenly seemed to realise the gravity of the situation. For if anyone was intent in bringing the USA into the war on Britain's side, it was America's crippled president, Franklin Delano Roosevelt.

'So this is it, Ian?' Godfrey said.

Fleming lowered his glass. 'I think so, sir. I don't think the Huns would go to these lengths without it being something big, really very big. The *Bismarck*, the *Prinz Eugen* are coming out of the Baltic at last and, as the Great Man said last week, it's not to stop a convoy filled to gunwhales with corned beef for the people of this country.'

Godfrey nodded his understanding and looked at the huge chart of the North Atlantic and North Sea which graced one wall of Room 39. 'The bulk of the Home Fleet is safe in Scapa Flow to the north there. We have various small task forces cruising off the coast to the south, west and one in the mid-Atlantic, bringing home a convoy. And there's one large one coming back from Murmansk in Russia. It's top secret but the Great Man has decided to help the Reds with some strategic goods before the shooting starts. Strange,' he mused as an afterthought, 'when Churchill has spent so much of his political life trying to eradicate communism. No matter. So, we've got the Home Fleet separated, but not too far apart and we have two convoys that the Hun might attack and destroy if he wants to achieve a quick propaganda victory without risking the *Bismarck* too much.' He paused, as if he didn't know how to continue, which was in reality the truth. Godfrey was not a man for drawing long-term conclusions. He was more at home on the quarterdeck of a fighting ship than in the rarified atmosphere of Intelligence.

The others took up the challenge, trying to outguess the Germans, while the messages continued to pour in. But for the most part they were disappointing. The Baltic was shrouded in fog and, although by flying – illegally – ever southern Swedish air space, RAF reconnaissance planes had managed to penetrate the area of Danzig, intense flak had prevented them getting low enough to take serial photographs.

As Ian Fleming concluded around midday, as Peggy the Wren, temporarily attached to the Admiralty – thanks to Fleming's influence with Godfrey – brought in sandwiches and pink gin, 'We're boxing in the dark, gentlemen. The Baltic is not going to reveal any of its secrets this day,' he announced, taking a sip of his pink gin and knowingly winking to Peggy. She blushed and fled, revealing that delightful bottom of hers beneath her tight serge skirt and reminding

Fleming that there were other perversions yet to come. The thought inspired him to add, 'But let's not be despondent, gentlemen. We know the *Bismarck's* out – one.' He ticked off the statement on one immaculately manicured finger. 'That she's after blood – two. And – three – she'll grab a quick victory somewhere or other before the Home Fleet can assemble and do a bunk for some close home base ... probably in Norway or occupied France.'

There was a mumble of agreement from the others, even from those who disliked or envied Fleming. But for once, he was wrong. Half an hour later, when they were on to their second pink gin, the usual grim-faced, armed RAF officer from Bletchley arrived, with his briefcase chained, as was customary, to his left wrist.

Hastily, they went through the complicated formalities and then, with the office door locked and the RAF flight lieutenant watching them suspiciously, hand poised on the holster of his revolver, Godfrey read out a message which was to be destroyed exactly sixty seconds after it had been seen. To a casual listener, it meant virtually nothing. But to them, it turned their world upside down.

It read: *'Lt Cdr Savage arrived Stockholm ... Urgent Blood and Iron ... Send Mossy to expedite. Hillgarth.'*

The silence was almost gravelike as Godfrey handed the message wordlessly back to the RAF officer. He wasted no time. Holding it above the nearest ashtray, he zipped his cigarette lighter and burned it before their eyes. Then, saluting, he snapped, 'I'll be on my way, gentlemen.'

Without another word, he marched across the office, unlocked the door and was gone, leaving them silent and unmoved like characters frozen into inactivity at the end of the third act of a fourth-rate melodrama...

Five

'E-boats, skipper,' the look-out shouted, above the steady throb of the old destroyer's engines. *'Starboard...'*

The young captain of HMS *Bulldog* heard the bearing only vaguely, for he had already seen the two lean white shapes. They were racing straight for the little convoy, their scrubbed woodwork and pre-war polished brass gleaming in the fitful rays of the morning sun now breaking through the surface fog. 'Bloody hell, that's torn it,' he cried. Next moment he was bent over the voice tube, yelling orders down from the bridge.

The gunlayers were on target almost immediately. But the Germans reacted even quicker. The twin twenty cannon opened fire. At a tremendous rate they pumped a solid wall of glowing white tracer shells at the old destroyer and the first of the merchant men behind the escort. Almost immediately, the *Bulldog* started to take casualties, as the rigging came tumbling down and the wireless mast fell in a shower of electric blue sparks. A fire control party went down in the lower desk, a nest of flailing arms and legs. Screams and yells for help rose from all sides. Suddenly the lower deck was running red with blood.

But now the A and B turrets were responding. The bigger four and a half inches cracked. The ship shuddered at the recoil. Spouts of angry white water hurtled upwards to left and right of the speeding crafts, their sharp prows knifing the water, throwing up combs of water. 'Lower the range,' the young skipper yelled desperately, as yet another vicious salvo of twenty millimetre automatic fire raked the destroyer: a thousand shells a minute running the length of the hull, ripping and gouging out the plates in sudden sparkling naked metal. *Bulldog* reeled dangerously.

But the skipper knew she was a tough old bugger. She could stand it. The E-boats, with their wooden hulls were a different kettle of fish. A lucky hit with one of the four and a half inch shells and that would be that. The Hun bugger wouldn't survive a minute.

Again, the two turrets fired. A burst of shells punched the leading E-boat. The German craft stopped. It was as if it had just run into an invisible stone wall. Next moment, steam and flames were escaping from its ruptured engine and she was sinking, with panic-stricken sailors throwing carley floats overboard or throwing themselves into the freezing water in which they wouldn't survive more than a few minutes.

Still the other E-boat kept up the attack. It swept round in a great angry curve, vanishing for a moment or two behind the sudden wall of flying water. For a moment the skipper of the *Bulldog* thought she was going to stop and pick up survivors of the other craft. That wasn't to be. A second later she came out of the fog of water, heading straight for the *Bulldog*, torpedo men, who had appeared out of nowhere, poised at her tilted bow.

The young skipper of the *Bulldog* didn't wait for the Germans to fire. Instead he yelled, 'Port seven,' in the same instant that the machine gunner in the open cage behind the bridge let loose with the round-barrelled, old-fashioned Lewis gun. Lead splattered off the leaping bow of the E-boat. One of the torpedo men flung up his arms dramatically, helplessly, a series of red buttonholes stitched abruptly across his chest, and disappeared over the side.

Instinctively, the other torpedo mate fired his deadly 'tin fish', filled with two tons of high explosive. It slid into the water. An excited flurry of bubbles. Then it was speeding towards the *Bulldog*. But already the aged British destroyer was pulling away to port.

Now the torpedo raced furiously towards its target, as if it had a mind of its own and was determined not to let the enemy escape. But that wasn't to be.

It hissed by the churning stern screws of the *Bulldog* by what seemed inches and hurried on. Behind the destroyer, its shattered mast almost touching the water as it swept round in that tight curve, the first of the little freighters, chugging along at the regulation convoy speed of eight knots, was not so nifty. Frantically its skipper tried to emulate the *Bulldog*'s manoeuvre. To no avail. The deadly torpedo struck its bow in mid-turn.

There was a blinding, electric flash of vivid violet flame. The freighter's bow seemed to leap out of the water. Next moment her back broke and she was sinking in two separate parts, the front end rearing up abruptly in a clifflike mess of shattered burning steel. A moment later and the second E-boat had broken off its attack and was surging away, audibly hitting each wave as it reached forty knots an hour, driving for the safety of the fog and Texel beyond...

That minor skirmish was the start of many that May day. German dive-bombers, the antiquated Stukas, easy meat for the British fighters, came over in swarms to fall out of the sky screaming, sirens going full out, to attack such coastal backwaters as Eastbourne, Southsea and the like. To what purpose no one seemed able to guess. At midday, off Withernsea in East Yorkshire, a run-down Victorian spa of no military value whatsoever, a German sub appeared and lobbed a few shells at the pier and what was left of the Victorian towers, where worthy middle-class citizens from Hull had once strolled and savoured the bracing sea air.

In London itself, the capital's air raid defences were repeatedly put on 'red alert'. Since the great German raid of 10 May, when 1,500 Londoners had died and double that number had been injured, the authorities had been expecting another attempt to put the capital out of action. Even the chamber of the House of Commons had been burned down to blackened walls and Churchill had wept. But the Germans, attacking everywhere, didn't chance heavy losses by attempting to bomb London once more. And it was this factor that caused the clever young men of Admiral Godfrey's Naval Intelligence section in Room 39 to continue to believe that these tremendously widespread German attacks were cover for the *Bismarck*'s foray into the open sea.

Still they were puzzled, and terribly worried. For if they came up with a definite statement on the *Bismarck*'s intentions, they knew this would influence their Lordships' deployment of the Home Fleet. As Admiral Godfrey, who had now taken to secreting a bottle of malt whisky in his office, to which he recoursed at regular intervals, remarked more than once, 'Gentlemen, we'll only get one bite of the cherry – and God help England and the Home Fleet if we make a mistake. Please bear that in mind in your deliberations.' And with that he would disappear into his own office for yet another sip of the whisky.

Thus it was, as more and more alarmist reports of German naval and air activity continued to pour in, the 'clever young men', as Godfrey liked to call his intelligence staff, mostly civilians in uniform, waited with growing impatience for the arrival of the 'Mossy' with its cargo from Stockholm.

Naturally they had looked up Savage in the Naval List and had soon found out that he had been captured the year before, imprisoned at Wesertimke and according to the 'protecting power', in this case the Swiss Red Cross, escaped from the POW camp a couple of months ago. But how he had gotten to Sweden still remained a mystery.

That 'urgent blood and iron', hadn't fooled them for very long either. '*Bismarck*, of course,' Montague, ex-lawyer and now a member of the 'clever young men', had exclaimed almost at once. 'Remember that speech he made back in the 1860s.'

'Actually, he said "iron and blood",' Fleming had objected a little petulantly that he had not made the discovery.

'Oh don't be such a fart-carrier, Ian,' Montague had snapped airily. 'This is not a bloody seminar on German history, you know. So, our man – Savage – knows something about Bismarck, and it can only be about the Hun ship. Why else would Stockholm request one of our Mosquitoes to bring him back tootsweet? The Mossy is hardly off the secret list, after all.'

When no one responded, the clever ex-lawyer looked around at the circle of glum and impatient faces and said, with forced cheerfulness, 'Gentlemen, there is nothing we can do, but wait for the Mossy and Commander Savage. In the meantime, I suggest we collect our dear chief and convince him to invite us to a slap-up lunch at White's. For my part, I'm heartily sick of whale meat and boiled potatoes.'

It was suggestion that was met by smiles on the part of the others, save Fleming, who would have dearly loved to have indulged himself in what he called a 'nooney'.

Thus those eager young men, mainstays of the Empire and upper-class system, ventured out into a bombed London, the shattered buildings peering through a fading fog of smoke turning the spring day into a weird November. They coughed in the acrid air as cinders wafted down like black snow. But the fact that the capital of the British Empire – 'all that red on the map' – was in such a sad state didn't seem to worry them much. They laughed at the elderly bobby, who naturally saluted them, guarding a smoking ruin, now emptied of anything of value. They hooted at the sight of a taxi-cab, with the great billowing balloon of gas on its roof in lieu of petrol to propel it, and enquired whether it was going to take off for Berlin that night in retaliation ... For basically, as clever as they were, they were careless people, born in the belief that things would always work out well for them and their kind. If their world was crumbling all around them, never to be restored, they didn't seem aware of it.

So they passed on their giddy, flippant way to the club, and five hundred or so miles away to the east, the *Bismarck* and its escort, the *Prinz Eugen*, sailed undetected through the Baltic narrows and then, gathering speed, headed for the safety of the Norwegian ports, from which they would sail to do battle with the 'Tommies' at last.

The scene was set, the actors were in place, the drama could commence...

BOOK FOUR

Defeat into Victory

BOOK FOUR

Defeat into Victory

One

Dawn broke cold, grey, vicious.

A surprisingly cruel wind – for that time of the year – tore across the Denmark Strait. It ripped at the waves with its white fingers. It hurled the freezing cold spray over the lookouts, huddled in layer upon layer of clothing. It was no better on the bridge of the cruiser *Norfolk*. The wind buffeted the bridge party. It tore the words from their mouths. They were forced to speak only when necessary and when they did, the icy air stabbed their lungs like a razor-sharp blade.

Still the cruiser ploughed on. The bow cleaved the green heaving waves, never-ending, it seemed, in their determination to slow the *Norfolk* down, as she unwittingly sailed to her doom.

The men were on their toes, despite the conditions and the danger. All of them, down to the youngest 'snotty' and rating knew the importance of their mission. The *Bismarck* and her escort the *Prinz Eugen* were out, heading for the 'blue water'. They had to find her and alert the leading ships of the Home Fleet before she managed to escape south. Breakfast, their only meal, had been cold greasy bacon, washed down with lukewarm milkless tea from flasks, though there had been a tot of rum. Now the captain had ordered the galley fires doused and the cooks on watch. Every available hand was needed on deck now. And the cooks, well-known throughout the senior service, as great moaners, obeyed without complaint.

On the bridge, the officers of the watch continued to scour the heaving grey horizon through their glasses, their eyes bloodshot with the strain. By now radar and radio were picking up enemy signals.

Back in Whitehall, the Admiralty could make little of them; as the captain of the *Norfolk* was informed in a terse signal, 'Colonel Bogey.' It was a strange form of communication from their Lordships, which puzzled the prim-and-proper young communications officer who brought the message to the skipper until the latter burst abruptly, and very surprisingly, into song, 'Bollocks and the same to you ... Where was the engine driver when the boiler burst ... They found his bollocks...' Thereupon he grinned and informed the startled youngster, who had thought the skipper had gone mad with the strain, 'It's all a cock-up,

Perkins. Nobody knows nothing...'

In the end it wasn't the *Norfolk*, but her sister ship the *Suffolk*, which first spotted the enemy. Cruising at a leisurely eighteen knots, the *Suffolk* saw them in mid channel. Instantly the radio operators bent over their desks, as up top they saw her in full detail: masts, funnels and huge guns, which spouted fire and smoke instantly.

The grey midday sky was torn apart by their elemental fury. One ... two ... three ... four ... Huge spouts of angry white water flailed upwards, and down below in the radio room, which shuddered like a live thing under the impact. The leading hand cried, 'God in frigging heaven ... it's the end of the frigging world...'

It wasn't. But to those who were there that May and who would live to tell their bloody and heroic tale, it almost seemed like that. The *Bismarck* had arrived. The battle had commenced...

'Here she comes now, chaps,' the RAF Controller announced over the tannoy system, which echoed metallically back and forth across Croydon Field. 'Right on time. Watch your noddles, you down there on the runway, *please*.'

Hastily the eager young officers of Naval Intelligence stepped back beyond the end of the flare-path.

One minute the Mosquito wasn't there, the next the beautiful wooden plane came hurtling down the runway at a tremendous speed, exhibiting why it could fly over the Reich totally unarmed; for the *Luftwaffe* hadn't a single fighter which could catch up with Britain's latest and most secret plane. Even Commander Fleming, the born cynic, was impressed. 'By jove, sir,' he exclaimed to Admiral Godfrey, 'doesn't she set a cracking pace,' and then they were submerged by the ear-splitting noise, as the RAF pilot throttled back and brought the twin-engined plane that had flown from Stockholm, with its all-important passenger, to a stop.

Now even before the little grey RAF utility truck could trundle out to the plane, the men of Naval Intelligence surged forward, eager to get a first look at the passenger hidden in the Mosquito's bomb-bay. Even Admiral Godfrey, despite his age, bulk and position, allowed himself to be taken with the mob of excited young officers.

A minute or two later, Savage was being helped out on to the tarmac, his legs still very shaky from the long tight trip, to face his eager interrogators. His features were gaunter than ever and there were two long lines etched deep about his mouth, indicating a man who had suffered a lot. But his eyes were his most striking features that May afternoon in Croydon.

They were naturally hard and aware, as they should be in a man who had suffered so much and had been near to death several times; but they were also puzzled, as if he couldn't understand these men, crowding around him, so eager, so well-fed, so content with life. It was as if Savage were asking, where have you lot been during the last years of the war ... how have you suffered ... where are your wounds?

But naturally the 'clever young men' of Admiral Godfrey's Naval Intelligence section didn't know. Even if they had, it would not really have concerned them. They had nothing to be ashamed of. Let lesser mortals go out and die heroically. It was their job to help win the war and, when that was done, to carry on running the Empire, as they and their kind had always done. Undoubtedly they would die in bed of old age; it was their due and privilege.

Admiral Godfrey thrust out his hand, while the others waited eagerly to start questioning the puzzled young man with the emaciated, bitter face.

'Glad to see you aboard once more, Savage,' the Admiral was saying as they started to move back to the waiting staff cars. 'We can't wait to hear what you have to tell us about the escape, your encounter with this Gestapo chap M—'

'Müller, sir.'

'Yes, Müller, and what he informed you about the *Bismarck*. How very odd indeed.' He helped Savage through the open door of the big Humber blue-painted staff car, while on the approach road a motorbike headed towards the little convoy of waiting staff cars, going all-out. 'I can't see why a person of that kind, the worse kind of Hun brute, should help us, Savage. Not for the life of me—'

'Do you think it was a plant, Savage?' Fleming cut in, sick of the Admiral's bumbling approach. 'Some kind of Nazi ploy – a very clumsy one, if it is, in my humble opinion – to mislead us once we knew that the *Bismarck* was on the high seas.' Fleming leaned forward impatiently, as if willing the other man to speak up and solve the mystery.

Savage looked at Fleming, his face full of contempt as he got a whiff of the expensive eau-de-Cologne that this fellow lieutenant-commander used. 'No, I don't think it is,' he said slowly, his disdain for the other man all too obvious. 'Why should he go to all that trouble to have me flown to Stockholm and have me delivered to the British Embassy. If that came out, surely he would have been in serious trouble with his own chief, Himmler?'

Fleming wasn't impressed by the argument. 'Perhaps that chinless wonder of an ex-chicken farmer' – he meant Himmler – 'might have been involved in the plot too.'

'Ian,' Godfrey cut his subordinate short. 'Let Commander Savage tell his story first. Then we can make some decisions about it, eh?'

But Savage was not fated to tell his strange tale yet and when he did, it would really be too late. For, in that instant, as the petty officer had engaged gear and was about to set off for the journey back to central London, followed by the rest, the naval dispatch rider daringly swerved across the road, one hand held up in stern command, crying above the racket kicked up by his BSA, 'STOP ... PLEASE ... STOP!'

'Silly bugger,' the petty officer cried, 'ain't even started yet. Want to frigging kill us all ... and the Admiral on board as well?'

But no one was listening to the petty officer's enraged outburst, not even Admiral Godfrey. They were all staring entranced at the dispatch rider, who had appeared out of nowhere and had had the temerity to stop them in this high-handed un-regulations manner. Not that the DR was concerned. He was fumbling in the leather pouch he wore around his neck. What he wanted was a small sealed flimsy, which he handed to the petty officer with the command, 'Give that to your senior officer, at once.'

Under other circumstances, the petty officer might have given the rating on the bike what he would have called 'a mouthful o' old buck'. But not now, he was too surprised. He took the flimsy and, turning with difficulty, gave it to Admiral Godfrey, who, in his turn, passed it on to Fleming with the words, 'If it's in clear, you read it, Ian. Left my spectacles in the office, dammit all.'

Hurriedly, while Savage watched without any apparent curiosity, Fleming opened the message printed on oilskin paper. He glanced at it and announced, 'It's in clear, sir ... Shall I read it aloud ... It's *very* important.'

'Pray do so, Ian.' He added then for the benefit of the driver, 'Close the partition, petty officer.'

'Sir,' the driver answered dutifully.

Fleming waited. Behind, in the other cars, the young men of Naval Intelligence wound down the windows and craned out their necks, curious to know why they hadn't moved off now they had Savage out of the plane.

Ian Fleming whistled softly and then he looked up. 'Admiral ... gentlemen,' he announced in a voice that he had once reserved for his odd appearances before the school in Eton Chapel, 'the *Hood* is about to engage the *Bismarck*...'

Two

'It's the *Hood* all right, Admiral,' the youngest officer on the bridge announced with the certainty of youth.

Admiral Lutjens remained undecided. He peered through the rolling low fog, while the rest of his middle-aged officers, who were too vain to wear glasses, did the same. Every now and again, he would catch a glimpse of the English squadron in the gleaming circles of his binoculars. 'Are you sure, *Herr Oberleutnant*?' he asked finally.

'*Jawohl, Herr Admiral*,' the officer replied promptly, blushing furiously for some reason known only to himself. 'It's the *Hood* all right. Can't mistake that silhouette, sir.'

'Famous last words,' Lutjens tried to grin, but failed miserably. But he thought the boy was right and there was no time to lose. What a great victory it would be, if he could knock out the pride of the English Navy at no cost to himself. He made up his mind. 'Run up the battle flag – and permission-to-fire signal flag,' he snapped. 'We fight.'

For a moment, the Admiral thought his middle-aged staff officers were going to open their mouths and cheer. After all, they had spent all their adult lives preparing for this moment; they were about to enter action at last. Instead they contented themselves with rapping out orders, making calculations and surveying the distance between themselves and the dark shapes on the tossing green horizon.

'*Fertig* ... *fertig* ... *fertig* ... ready ... ready ... ready.' From all sides the eager shouts came, signifying that the various divisions of the great battleship were ready for action.

Lutjens did the expected thing: the privilege of the fleet commander. 'Stand by to open fire,' he commanded. There was no sense of urgency or triumph in his voice at that moment. Instead he was doubtful, hesitant. Behind him one of the senior mates chortled happily, 'Stand by for the waltz, girls.' Lutjens frowned. How easy they were taking it.

He flashed a glance at the glowing of his complicated gold chronometer, given to him by the Führer himself. Very carefully he noted the time. It was Central European Time, zero five hundred hours and fifty-two minutes. 'Eight minutes to six on a May morning in the year, 1941,' he whispered to himself, knowing he would never forget that time as long as he lived. For perhaps it mark-ed ... He hesitated. Dare he say the words aloud? He did. 'The end of the British Empire.'

Next moment, all doubts forgotten, he yelled at the top of his voice, *'FEUER FREI*!'

'They're hoisting the open fire ... open fire flags, sir,' the young officer cried across to Rear Admiral Holland. Hastily the latter focused his binoculars. Below him the smoke from his own B-gun turret was drifting away. The *Hood* did not have the best of gun platforms, but Holland was not slowing down to give Guns, his gunnery officer, the kind of stability he needed for accurate shooting. That would have been too risky, especially as the *Bismarck* was within firing range.

Carefully he counted off three seconds until the *Hood*'s first tremendous salvo detonated. They were firing at the *Bismarck*'s running mate, the *Prinz Eugen*; for it was Holland's guess that if the *Eugen* was seriously hurt, the *Bismarck*, deprived of its escort, would make a run for it. At least, he hoped she would.

'Thar they blow,' some rating yelled, carried away by the excitement of it all.

'They're on target,' someone else cried, as the deckmen tensed for the result of the

240

first strike.

Glued to his glasses, Holland watched as the first huge shell exploded to the starboard of the *Bismarck*. A miss. The knuckles of his hands holding the glasses whitened even more, the only sign of his frustration. The second strike was a miss, too. Again the shell fell between the two German ships, but closer. Holland could see how even the *Bismarck* trembled under the impact of the near miss. 'Damn and blast,' he cursed through gritted teeth. 'Hit the bugger, will you!'

Next moment the third shell struck home. It hit the *Prinz Eugen*. A burst of intense black smoke rose, turning into a cloud several hundred feet high in an instant. In its centre a sudden cherry-red fire started to rage furiously. In its blinding ruddy glare, Holland, his eyes narrowed to slits, could see the *Eugen*'s radio masts come tumbling and slithering down to the deck in a series of angry blue and pink sparks. Almost instantly the German ship began to lose speed.

'We've hit the sod,' Holland heard himself shouting, as if he were listening to someone else. 'WE'VE HIT THE *EUGEN*!'

Now the Home Fleet, the greatest in the world, was beginning to close in on the in-solent German intruders, who were making this cheeky attempt (so the British thought) to tackle the Royal Navy in its own backyard. The main Home Fleet had left its berth in Scapa Flow, sailed around the north of the British Isles in a westwards direction and was desperately sailing all out to cut off the enemy's escape route back to France, if that was the direction in which the *Bismarck* and *Prinz Eugen* would flee.

To the west of the Home Fleet, the two battleships HMS *Rodney* and *Ramilles* had taken up a back-up position in order to stop any attempt by the fugitive enemy to make a dash for the North Atlantic and the general direction of the American coast.

In the meantime, the *Hood* Force and the two cruisers, *Sheffield* and *Norfolk*, continued to engage the *Bismarck* and the *Prinz Eugen*, now waiting for the torpedo bombers from the aircraft carriers in the south to arrive and put the finishing touches to the destruction of these impudent Huns, who had dared to enter British waters like this.

The Bismarck's Last Voyage

Indeed the Admiralty started to feel complacent about the outcome of the running battle. The pressure started to ease. It was a foregone conclusion, wasn't it? The Huns could not escape; they were faced with too much British firepower.

At Naval Intelligence they were not so sure. By now Savage was beginning to open up, though as yet they couldn't quite believe his strange tale. Godfrey had told his officers privately during the several breaks they had been forced to make in their interrogation of the escaped officer (Savage, for all his tough appearance, was at the end of his tether, weakened by the year in captivity, his escape and the beatings afterwards): 'In view of what the man's been through, we can expect him to be a little barmy. Who wouldn't under those circumstances, poor sod.'

It was a sentiment with which the others agreed, save Fleming. He remained hard, cynical and sceptical. 'Poor sod he might be, sir,' he remarked acidly. 'But if we're to accept even part of his downright crazy story – this business with the head of the Gestapo,' he'd added with a snort of contempt, 'Savage must have worked with the enemy, don't you think? Collaboration, if you like to call a spade a bloody shovel?'

The others had not risen to the bait. Indeed some of them, like Montague, had given Fleming looks of annoyance, which seemed to indicate that he should keep his damned prejudiced opinions to himself. But Fleming being Fleming had not even noticed. Invariably he was right and the others were wrong.

But as fantastic as Savage's story about his pact with Gestapo Müller was, the Admiralty were eager to know the details. If the Hun was really a secret communist working for the Bolsheviks, he would be in a position to deliver to them top secret German information. And it was a typical Russian ploy to involve a neutral third country in their devious plots. That country would think it was working in its own interests; in fact, it would be indirectly working for the Russians. So with a war impending between Soviet Russia and Nazi Germany, what better way to paralyse or seriously damage the German Navy before it could be used again in Russia, than to let the British do the job for the Russians. For the more far-sighted of their

Lordships at the Admiralty, this could be one logical explanation behind the strange agreement between Müller and the insignificant escaped British naval officer.

'You see, gentlemen,' Savage had explained right at the start of his account, 'Müller had me by the short and curlies, if you'll excuse my French. He was going to keep the woman – a Polish girl – who had helped me escape from the farm as security. As long as I promised to tell you and no one else about the *Bismarck*, so that he would not risk his own thick neck, she would be safe.' Savage frowned uneasily at the memory of that meeting, 'And if things went well, we could meet again after the war.'

'Oh my God,' Fleming had moaned softly in mock exasperation, 'we'll have Vera Lynn on next warbling that sentimental twaddle of hers.'

'Shut up, Ian,' Godfrey had snapped, for once losing patience with his chief assistant. Typical sailor of the old school, a no-nonsense type – all the same he had commanded men for long enough to know when someone was speaking from the heart, and Savage was certainly doing that. 'Let the man speak, will you.'

Now Savage had finished speaking; his interrogation was over and, drained of energy as he was, he was hanging on strictly out of a sense of duty and the knowledge that if he made a balls-up of this business, it would be a totally defenceless Elena who would suffer.

Thus it was that when Fleming slowly began to think of the coming delights with the obedient and willing little Wren, Peggy, that Godfrey put down his afternoon tea and gobbled his last chocolate biscuit before anyone else had the temerity to take it. With an air of finality in his voice, he asked. 'All right, Savage, we're going to get you back to your billet soon, so that you can get a good bath and as much shuteye as you need.'

'Thank you, sir,' Savage said with unaccustomed humility, for he had grasped that he was in the power of people who would use him as long as they needed him and then get rid of him swiftly and quietly. If he were ever going to see Elena again, and now that had become a priority in his life, he would have to play this clever game. He already knew far too much about what was going on on both sides of the pond. For the time he would play the game with his cards held tightly to his chest. So he controlled his anger, and added with seeming gratitude, 'That's awfully kind of you, sir.'

Godfrey beamed. He had obviously assessed his man correctly. 'Let us assume that the *Bismarck* will soon have to make a run for it – the Admiralty tells me that she and her sister ship, the *Prinz Eugen* are under fire from our guns – where will she head for? Now this is vital. We can't waste time and ships searching all over the show for her, once she breaks and runs.' He looked hard at the other man.

Savage was ready with his answer. 'Müller, sir, told me that he knew that for certain, from two different sources. Grand Admiral Raeder's HQ in Berlin and even better from his own Gestapo officials in France, who seemingly know everything that's going on at service headquarters there.' He paused and noted the power he had suddenly achieved. They were hanging on his every word, even that supercilious snob, Fleming.

'Go on,' Godfrey prompted him.

But before Savage could continue, the door burst open and a red-faced admiral, his tunic wide open, his tie askew, eyes popping out of his head like those of a man demented, tormented beyond all reason, cried aghast, 'The *Hood* ... the Huns have sunk the *Hood*...'

Three

The *Prinz Eugen*'s second salvo came howling in like some great speeding express through a silent midnight station. The noise was tremendous, awe-inspiring terrifying. This time the second barrage didn't miss. The three huge shells slammed into the smoke-shrouded *Hood*. The main mast was hit. It came roaring down. Sparks and shattered metal flew everywhere. Shrapnel scythed lethally across the debris-littered main deck. Men and metal went down, ripped apart effortlessly. Everywhere there were dead and dying men, writhing and squirming in their death agonies in pools of dark-red, smoking blood.

The deck stowage caught light immediately. Within seconds the flames were crackling and blazing as high as the stacks. An instant later, the wind fanned the flames into a gigantic blowtorch of all-consuming fire. It swept the length of the huge deck, burning all in front. Ratings were turned into scorched, charred crouched pygmies in a flash. Boats went up like tinderwood. The grey wartime paint bubbled and sizzled like the symptons of some loathsome skin disease. In a flash all was horror and sudden violent death.

Still the great doomed ship came on in its final ride of death. It was as if nothing could stop her. Even in her death throes she was intent on closing with the enemy. After all, hadn't this been the reason for her creation so long before?

It was just the target that the *Bismarck* needed. What better kind of 'blooding' for this totally new ship than the destruction of the pride of the Royal Navy – HMS *Hood*? Lutjens, on the bridge of the *Bismarck*, didn't hesitate. He made some swift mental calculations. He knew where and when to strike. There would be no excuse for the gunners this time, as there had been at that ill-fated *Battle of Jutland* in 1916. This time it was going to be a German triumph; it *had* to be!

Above Lutjens on the bridge, Fire Control made their calculations. Hastily they relayed them to an impatient, nervous Lutjens. He'd have the honour of issuing the decisive fire order. It was going to ensure his place in naval history, that of the commander who had sunk the *Hood*.

But it wasn't going to be all that easy. Even as he made his decision, the enemy shells raked the *Bismarck*. Great gouts of water shot up to starboard. Metal sang through the air. Lutjens yelped and grabbed a stanchion. He felt a stinging pain in his forehead. He reached up with a shaky hand. His cap had vanished. Something wet and warm was trickling down the side of his face. He had been hit. It was his own blood. The damned Tommies were not going to go down without a fight. Now it was to be a duel to the death.

He shook his head. Everything came back into focus once more. Holding up his hand to staunch the blood, he started to cry out his orders in a voice that he hardly recognised as his own; his voice was that shaky. But even as he determined to finish off the *Hood*, Admiral Lutjens knew that that would be the end of the attack. Thereafter, the Tommies would be after him like a pack of vengeful bloodhounds. They'd want revenge all right. He'd have to make a run for it and pray that he'd reach Brest before those English hounds of hell caught up with him

He made his decision. 'Elevate A and B,' he commanded. Almost immediately the great steel turret hummed with electricity and began to swing round in the direction of the enemy. 'Maximum height ... plunging fire ... two salvoes.' Suddenly he felt, as if someone had opened an unseen tap in his body. All his energy seemed to flow out. He felt lethargic, as if he had just pounded the ribs of some hot whore in a mattress polka.

Then it happened.

The huge shells – one, two, three – plunged down at a tremendous speed. They sliced right through the *Hood*'s deck armour. They cut the steel plates like a hot knife through butter. Ammo commenced exploding. It was suddenly like Bonfire Night. Shells flew in every direction in a crazy pattern of multi-coloured light. The *Hood* started to tremble. It was an unbelievable sight: the enormous steel ship quivering frighteningly. The men on board trembled too.

On the bridge of the cruiser *Norfolk* they viewed the sudden transformation of the sky from grey to violet, to brilliant red and then to a smoke-distorted grey, once more with total bewilderment. What was going on a couple of sea miles away? What in God's name was happening to the *Hood*?

A moment later they found out. To their horror. Suddenly, the grey sky turned to livid, awe-inspiring burning fire. The *Hood* gave a violent shudder. Like a savage animal caught unexpectedly by a hunter's bullet and taken by surprise as its hindlegs start to weaken and give way.

A hellish boom. The *Hood* was shrouded by thick grey smoke. The cloud rose higher and higher. It commenced to lay a shroud over the dying vessel. Here and there, bursts of vivid cherry-red flames. That frightening, awesome trembling commenced once more. Plates sprung. Pieces of derricks clattered to the tilting deck or showered the water to both sides. Another mast came tumbling down. The ship's plane slithered slowly but inevitably along the deck. Slowly, almost comically, it went over the side and floated there for a few moments. Then the sea snatched it greedily and it disappeared. Now the *Hood* started to break apart.

Open-mouthed and gawping like village yokels, the men on the *Norfolk* watched the great ship go to her doom. Surely, their faces spoke, it couldn't be happening to the *Hood*? But it was.

She was racked by another terrible explosion. There was the wrenching, ear-splitting grinding of metal being ripped apart by force. Like some great grey whale surfacing for air, the whole of her bow rose higher and higher. Desperate tiny figures slithered its length, frantically fighting for a hold. In vain. They disappeared into the white frothy maelstrom below. A man dived from a shattered derrick. It was a beautiful performance like that given by some pre-war fleet champion before a crowd of admiring matelots. His dive failed. He missed his aim. Instead of the water, he hit the deck like a sack of wet cement – and burst open.

Now the watchers could hear the faint sad cries for help. *'Mercy ... God help me ... Don't leave me mates, I can't see ... HELP ... MOTHER...'* It was almost over now. Here and there the watchers shielded their eyes, turned away, heads bent, as if they could no longer stand the sight.

Abruptly, the bow plunged down again. Water shot up out of the centre of the fog of smoke. Higher ... higher ... hundreds of feet into the grey sky. More and more panic-stricken ratings flung themselves hopelessly into the freezing water. They knew they wouldn't survive more than a couple of minutes in that arctic sea. Perhaps they wanted to die quickly. Now the men of the *Hood* were beginning to die fast ... by their score, the hundred ... the thousand.

On the *Norfolk* hardened petty officers sighed. Those were their shipmates they'd gotten pissed with in Pompey, visited knocking shops with in Shanghai and Hong Kong, with whom they had paraded in half a score of glittering ceremonies all over the Empire 'showing the flag'. *Their oppos!* Now they were dying only a mile or so away and there wasn't one fucking thing they could fucking well do about it...

Lutjens pushed back his hair and wiped the sweat off his furrowed forehead. It was a ploy to dab his eyes at the same time; they were full of tears. It was the enemy dying, he knew that. But at the same time he was watching the end of a great ship and, like all sailors, that was something he hated to see. In the end all men, whatever their nationality and whether they were at war with one another or not, who went down to the sea felt the tragedy of a dying ship. This time Lutjens didn't give the order for the salvo which he knew would be the *Bismarck*'s last to fire at the dying *Hood*. He left that target task to 'Guns'.

Once more the *Bismarck*'s cannon boomed. A great swish. The howl of ton-heavy shells rushing across the sky. The terrible wind that swept the deck, as if the Devil himself wanted to wipe them all off the face of the earth into his evil clutches.

For what seemed an eternity, nothing happened. Had the *Bismarck*'s shells failed to explode? They hadn't. Next to him a hearty junior officer who had just come up from below to enjoy the spectacle, cried, 'Holy straw sack ... just cast your glassy orbs on that ... *fer Chrissake!*'

A violent sheet of flame. It shot hundreds of feet high. A tremendous crash. Great white combers of water rushed towards the doomed ship. Startlingly forty-two thousand tons of steel started to disintegrate before their shocked gazes. The pride of the Royal Navy simply blew apart. One moment the *Hood* was there; the next she had gone, as if she had never even existed.

Metal showered the sea. The waves boiled in crazy fury. The oil slick caught light. Swiftly the tide of burning oil swept forward. It engulfed the men attempting to swim for it. Those on the carley floats didn't escape either. Their little craft were turned into instant death traps. Everywhere dying men pleaded with their God for mercy. But there was no mercy for the poor pathetic burning, drowning creatures. This day God was looking the other way.

Slowly, but surely the screams, the pleas, the curses against fate were submerged and muffled by the great cloud of thick black oil-tinged smoke which now arose until nothing more could be heard. On the *Norfolk*, the suddenly subdued matelots were glad. It gave them a moment's respite from the horror.

On the *Bismarck*, the men, too, were stunned. But not for long. Suddenly, the thought ran from man to man as if by some sort of naval bush telegraph: we've destroyed the pride of the English Navy! A wave of overwhelming ecstatic joy swept through the great German battleship. It went from division to division, deck to deck, mess to mess, right down to the sweating stokers in the bowels of the engine room. Suddenly discipline and strict military protocol were forgotten. Men embraced. Rank was forgotten. Officers shook hands, clapped petty officers on the shoulders, shouted joyously at humble ratings. They were like men seeing each other for the very first time, bringing some wondrous tiding.

The *Kriegsmarine*'s iron discipline, worse than that of the Royal Navy, based on the lash, relaxed for a few moments. Those who possessed illegal 'flatmen', hip-pocket bottles of schnapps and *Korn* liquor broke them out and started toasting victory and this was the end of the terrible war. Others ran back and forth wildly. They punched the air, slapping shipmates across the back, 'Good old shitting *Bismarck*,' they cried exuberantly. 'We knew she'd shitting well do it ... That'll teach that drunken sod, Churchill. *Himmel, Arsch und Amerika*! ... Now he can go and stick his Yankee cigar up his fat Tommy arse, eh!'

Men sang. Others, drunk on joy and schnapps, danced. Their comrades cheered. They made obscene gestures. There was wild talk of vaseline and bunks! They blew wet kisses. *Obermaat* Hansen, old, horny and totally depraved, gave one of his celebrated tuneful farts, modulated carefully to sound

256

like *'Deutschland uber Alles'*. Drunks attempted to stand to attention to the sound of the national anthem coming from Hansen's well-endowed musical arse. They fell flat on their faces instead.

Up on deck in 'officers' country' the celebrations were more subdued. But they celebrated all the same. 'God in heaven,' the junior officers chortled. 'Think of the tin' – they meant decorations for valour – 'the girls ... girls with flowers. It'll be Christmas every day ... roses all the way. Lads, we're going home to mother. Hurrah.'

Suddenly and strangely, Lutjens no longer seemed able to enjoy his crew's joy. Abruptly he felt a sense of foreboding, as if he had been found guilty of a nameless crime and had to be punished. He knew not why.

An hour later, he signalled Raeder in Berlin, 'Have sunk battle-cruiser *Hood*. Another battleship damaged and in retreat. Two heavy cruisers now shadowing. Fleet Commander.' The message seemed to reflect his new mood. Lutjens had just announced a great victory, soon to be celebrated wildly throughout the Reich. But he suddenly took no joy in it.

Half an hour later he signalled Raeder once more. Now his sense of triumph had vanished completely. The signal was sombre. It read:

257

1. Engine Room 4 out of action.
2. Port stokehold leaking. But can be held. Bows leaking severely.
3. Cannot make more than eighteen knots.
4. Two enemy radio scanners noted.
5. Intend to run for St Nazaire. No loss of men.

Fleet Commander.

The wild intoxication of victory was past. Cold realism had taken over. Admiral Lutjens now had no illusions about what was to come. The Tommies had lost their *Hood*. They would make him pay for that. He had studied the English ever since he had been a teenage cadet. He knew as much about the Royal Navy as he did of his own *Kriegsmarine*. The English never gave up.

He had to make his escape now. There was no other alternative. Otherwise he was doomed. He ordered the retreat – and the escape.

Majestic, but a lot slower now, the great German ship sailed into the grey unknown. Behind her she left an empty sea. It tossed back and forth in its cold-green intensity. Far off the shadows moved too. But alone in that great watery waste there were three men – three men only – the sole survivors of the HMS *Hood*...

Four

Death came to the *Bismarck* on the morning of Tuesday, 27 May, 1941. From Friday onwards, the British Home Fleet, thirsty to avenge those who had destroyed the *Hood*, had been hunting the *Bismarck* frantically. After all, the prestige of the senior service was at stake. It was no use an official Admiralty spokesman announcing to a shocked and grieving British public: 'And which of her great-hearted company would have been asked to be left behind on a day like this? God was very merciful to them. Their end was instantaneous and their fight an honest one in the greatest cause for which a sailorman ever put to sea.' Even Churchill, the only wartime leader on any side who felt anything for the suffering of his people, wasn't satisfied. 'They,' he meant the dead *Hood* crewmen, 'want revenge, not sentiment. Action this day. Get that *Bismarck* bastard!'

From all quarters the great ships converged on the *Bismarck*, as she twisted back and forth in intricate patterns and manoeuvres in an attempt to outwit her fiendish pursuers. For a while luck was on her side. The weather closed in and once, for as long as fifteen hours, the British ships lost contact. But with two aircraft carriers involved in the greatest chase of the war, she was found again. A coastal command flying boat spotted the *Bismarck* on the morning of 25 May. Thereafter the British never lost contact again.

By now Lutjens was a worried man. At first he felt he could throw off the two old British cruisers shadowing him. With the weather and the poor quality radar with which the British ships were equipped, he felt he had a good chance of reaching the protection of the French coast before the fireworks really started. But the information, culled from tapped British radio signals, that he had been sighted from the air, changed the situation considerably.

Now things really started to go wrong. He ordered Captain Brinckmann of the *Prinz Eugen* to take up station in front of the *Bismarck* to minimise damage if the enemy came within gunnery range. But nerves right at the top were rattled. Brinckmann made a mess of the tactic. They almost collided and for a while Bismarck's steering mechanism jammed. Thereafter Lutjens retired to his day cabin and had three swift schnapps until his hands ceased trembling. Thereafter he washed his face and stared at himself in the washbasin mirror. The face of a dead man stared back at him. He looked away hastily.

By now the distance between the *Bismarck* and her pursuers, the two old British cruisers, had been reduced to 120 miles. The minutes to that final confrontation were ticking away rapidly.

Lutjens, glum, unable to raise a smile for his staff officers, which he knew was fatal – a commander must always radiate confidence – let *Prinz Eugen* go on on her own. Perhaps the British would follow her. They didn't. They continued their pursuit of the *Bismarck*. The Admiral started to despair.

Now the British, with the *Bismarck* only a hundred miles away and the aircraft carriers on station, began to apply the pressure. The British Commander, Admiral Tovey, ordered the ancient torpedo bombers from the aircraft carrier *Victorious* into action. The 'stringbags', obsolete even before the war, were to slow the giant German battleship down even more. Then the ships would finish her off with gunfire, once they came within range.

In patchy cloud the British came in to the attack. The gunners on the *Bismarck* spotted them immediately when they broke cloud cover. They threw up a tremendous wall of burning steel. The whole port and starboard sides of the German battleship erupted with fire. Still the pilots pressed on, wave-hopping, slowed down even more by the 'tin fish' slung between the wheels of their fixed undercarriage. A plane was hit. It slammed down into the waves, turned turtle and lay there wallowing in the swell. No one got out.

The doomed squadron kept on. They seemed to be passing through a network of flame and smoke. Time and time the brave young pilots in their ancient planes disappeared into the smoking inferno. Yet they always emerged again. The lead plane got within striking distance. The pilot didn't hesitate. He fired his tin fish. The lightened Swordfish rose a good fifty feet into the air. Next moment the torpedo plopped to the waves and was up and running, heading straight for the *Bismarck*.

On the bridge Lutjens watched the wash as it sped towards the battleship, his hands clutching his binoculars turned into white-knuckled claws. He blinked. The torpedo had struck home. There was the great hollow boom of steel striking steel. The ship shuddered as the charge went off. Lutjens prayed fervently. His prayers were answered. The *Bismarck* steamed on, apparently untouched by the explosion at her bows.

As the surviving attack bombers turned to fly to their carrier before their fuel ran out, Lutjens forced himself to address the crew over the tannoy system. He boasted weakly that his ship had shot down twenty-seven British planes. It was a lie and even the stokers toiling in the bowels of the *Bismarck* knew it. They wiped their faces with their grease rags and whispered to each other, 'The old man's lost his nerve. He's beginning to cream his skivvies.'

Lutjens had. As soon as the announcement was over, he radioed Berlin to say that he was abandoning his attempt to lead his pursuers into a line of U-boats off St Nazaire, which was being hastily prepared by Doenitz. The latter raged and cursed to his young staff. '*Typisch!* What kind of piggery is this? The man ought to be in charge of a bimboat!'

Now a strange mood of apprehension and fatalism swept over the ship. They seemed to sense, even the dullest of the crew, that somehow their fate had been sealed. From being the terror of the sea, they had become a fugitive, hunted everywhere with every man's hand against them. Those who had charts kept looking at the French coast, trying to work out how long it would take the *Bismarck* to reach safety before the buck-teethed Tommies caught up with them.

Lutjens, not a religious man by any means, kept to his day cabin and prayed, and at the same viewed the weather, hoping fervently that God would make it break for the worse and give him one more chance to get away. More than once he thought of the fate of the *Hood*. Then he shuddered violently and had to get up and help himself to yet another stiff drink, his hand trembling violently, almost out of control. 'In three devils' name,' he moaned. 'When will it all end? When?'

In Room 39, they felt the same. By now Godfrey's 'clever young men' were hollow-eyed and shaky from too much black coffee, helped down by hidden sips of whisky and the Navy's favourite, pink gin. The Intelligence men simply couldn't relax. Even Fleming tried to take his mind off the great chase by thoughts of Peggy, the Wren, who wandered in and out at odd intervals, but he couldn't quite pull it off. He filled his mind with visions of her in various sexual poses. But they didn't work. Always, he came back to the 'bloody *Bismarck*', as he was now calling the German ship.

Savage was the only man who did not seem outwardly affected by the furore, the constant excited comings and goings, the incessant jingle of the phones, the messengers. He sat in the corner near the polished coal scuttle – which Peggy brought in filled and burnished every morning, bending low so that Fleming had full advantage of her black-stockinged legs – wrapped up in a cocoon of his own thoughts. Now no one seemed particularly concerned with him; he had served his purpose and they were fully occupied with the details of the running battle between the *Bismarck* and the Home Fleet.

Savage had other things on his mind. All his life he had been a loner. Then Elena had come into his life. But for such a brief time. Now he was tormented by the feeling that he might have lost her for good and he'd have to return to that solitary existence, where his only love – his only life – was the Royal Navy. But what could he do about it? Was there some way that he could exert pressure on Gestapo Müller to ensure that whatever the outcome of the current battle, she'd survive?

Naturally Müller was now open to blackmail. His treachery could be revealed. But would the British authorities allow that? Looking at the clever faces all around him of men who knew how to use anybody and everybody to their own advantage, Savage felt not. Gestapo Müller's treachery would be used in due course for some more important matter than the life – or death – of a lone Polish girl. Suddenly Savage realised, as all sensitive people do some time or other in wartime, that he was not important. The 'big picture', as the brass always calls the main issue, is what counts, not their petty lives with their petty worries and concerns. The brass pays lip service to the needs of the 'little man', but it is that, merely lip service.

Savage dropped his head and Montague, glancing momentarily in his direction knew instinctively what was going through the ex-POW's mind. 'Yes, chum,' he said to himself, 'one way or another, we're all bloody expendable...'

Admiral Lutjens had come to the same realisation, too. The Führer's signal, which he now held in a trembling hand, his eyes glazed with alcohol, though it could have been tears, made it clear that he was dispensable. It read, COME WHAT MAY, THE *BISMARCK* MUST ACHIEVE GLORY. UNDERSTOOD. LONG LIVE GERMANY! LONG LIVE OUR HOLY CAUSE!

The message had been read out to the crew – he could not bring himself to do it personally. There had been a few forced cheers. But not many. The men had understood Hitler's intention, just as he had. They were going to be sacrificed for the prestige of the National Socialist Reich. There would be no surrender. They would fight to the end and go down with their ship. Then Germany's honour would be satisfied. No one would give a damn about the hundreds of dead young men and their grieving relatives back home. They were merely cannon fodder, that's all.

Now captains of British ships in lost little ports, remote convoy duty, settling-down trials all over the North Atlantic slipped away unofficially from their assigned duties and tried to help in the search. These old forgotten skippers, who would never be promoted beyond their present command, smelt a fight. Signal after signal reached the C-in-C Admiral Tovey asking for permission to help find the *Bismarck*'s exact location and the Admiral felt he could do nothing to stop them.

The aircraft carriers closed in, too. It was against standard operation procedure for the lightly armed and armoured carriers to come within striking distance of a battleship. But now no one dare stop their skippers. It was said that everywhere stokers, trying to feed their engines to gain impossible speeds, were collapsing from heat stroke and exhaustion. Still the chase continued. For now everyone wanted to be in at the kill.

Now the end was near for the *Bismarck*. Yet

her fate was still not finally sealed. The weather started to worsen. There was a rising north-westerly wind and an increasing swell. It was becoming ever more difficult for the 'shadows', the great four-engined Sunderland flying-boats of Coastal Command, to keep on station. Tovey ordered his surface units to close up, whatever the risk, and not lose sight of the *Bismarck*. The result was that the HMS *Sheffield* soon received a blast from the *Bismarck*'s fifteen-inch guns. Like some tormented, cornered savage beast, the *Bismarck* was lashing out at anyone who came too close.

Still the destroyers went streaking in, a great white bone at their teeth. A profusion of torpedoes slid from their bows. Three hit. The *Bismarck* shuddered visibly and later the destroyer captains swore they heard her groan like some mortally wounded beast. An hour later the captain of the *Norfolk* Signalled: 'Enemy in sight twelve miles to the south of me ... Tin hats on.'

Minutes later *Rodney* followed with a similar report: 'Enemy sighted.' It was then that the C-in-C caught his first glimpse of the enemy. Veiled in the distant rainfall, a thick squat ghost of a ship, very broad in the beam was coming straight for him. Hastily he pulled on his 'tin hat' and was drenched with rain water for his pains. Admiral Tovey didn't even notice. Already his ships were beginning to pound their target. The *Bismarck* commenced returning fire: thin orange streaks cutting the grey squally rain. 'Battle bowlers on ... on the bridge,' Tovey ordered automatically, not taking his glasses off the enemy ship for one instant. 'Here we go chaps. Nelson expects and all that...'

Five

The tension had been too much for Fleming. He needed relief from the constant nail-biting of the long chase which was now going into the third day. All that time he and the rest of Room 39 had existed on black coffee, pink gin and biscuits. By now his every nerve was tingling electrically; and ever since he had first discovered the pleasures of sex at Eton while he had been a member of POP, he knew there was one capital remedy against nervous tension – what he called, 'a good rollicking bit of pokey-hokey!'

He had caught Peggy, the little Wren, as she bent down in the cellars to fill the burnished coal scuttle with the morrow's fuel. He had taken her completely by surprise. Naturally she had not screamed when he had crept up behind her and whipped up her skirts and then pressed himself against her, with, 'Now look, darling, what I've brought you.' She let out a little whimper.

It was the whimper which had caught

270

Savage's attention, as he had strode back and forth along the empty corridor above, lined with the oil painting of naval worthies in heavy wigs, striking the usual martial poses. Savage, as nervous and tense as Fleming – though for very different reasons – knew immediately what the whimper signified. Throwing his own concerns to the wind, he crept down the dark creaking old stairs that dated back to the eighteenth century to be confronted with the sight of Lieutenant-Commander Fleming, with his trousers around his ankles, prepared to enter the Wren, who was protesting but, all the same, had obligingly placed her hands on her knees to start the shock, as Fleming commanded, 'Prepare to stand by for boarders ... ha, ha.'

For a moment Savage was dumbstruck. He hadn't needed a crystal ball to know what had been going on between the two of them. He had seen the looks that had passed between them every time she had entered Room 39. But he hadn't thought it right that an officer of Fleming's rank and experience should be fornicating, against King's Regulations, with a Wren, who was perhaps half his age and pretty vulnerable at that.

Even before he had decided what to do, he heard himself say sharply, 'What's going on here, for God's sake? What's your ruddy game, Fleming, eh?'

The Wren jumped up. He could see the soft flesh of her plump buttocks shudder. She gasped just as Fleming's erection began to wither. A moment later the two of them were frantically grabbing at their underclothing to cover up their nakedness.

For a long moment there was a heavy silence, broken only by the hectic breathing of the two lovers, caught by surprise. Then, with his flies done up in part, Fleming snapped in his best haughty manner: 'Who the hell do you think you are, Savage – talking to me like that?' His thin face, with its broken nose, flushed a livid purple and automatically Savage clenched his right fist as if he were prepared to defend himself if Fleming came any closer. But he didn't. Instead he waited until the Wren had finished adjusting her skirt, not noticing that both her precious black stockings were badly laddered and beyond repair. Fleming nodded. Wordlessly, head bowed, face flushed with shame, she squeezed by Savage, as Fleming snorted, 'What a damned middle-class prig you are, Savage. Besides what right have you to interfere in my affairs?' His eyes flashed. 'Who knows just how pukka you are with your Gestapo Müller and supposed escape—'

'Shut up,' Savage Cut in coldly, fully in

272

control of himself. 'Remember the position I've just found you in.'

'One witness is no witness, may I remind you.'

'No, with your reputation. Who do you think would believe you? You've blotted your copybook all too often. Just keep away from that Wren.' Suddenly the thought of Elena flashed through Savage's mind. She'd been abused like the silly little Wren: aT every man's beck-and-call, without any recourse to justice and protection. 'Someone has to look after vulnerable girls like that.'

'Join the frigging Salvation Army,' Fleming was desperate to launch an attack – till he saw the look on Savage's emaciated face and changed his mind. Instead he contented himself with doing up the rest of his flies, saying softly, almost as if to himself as he did so, 'You'll bloody well regret this, Savage, believe me.' With that he was gone...

The end was near for the *Bismarck*. If the tension was still mounting in London, it had almost disappeared at the scene of action. The British, under the supervision of Admiral Tovey, knew they couldn't lose now. The odds against the dying *Bismarck* were overwhelming; it was only a matter of time before she went down now. In the *Bismarck* the mood was one of resignation. At the

range she was being engaged, her Krupp armour was being holed like Swiss cheese. She was taking hit after hit.

By noon, a British salvo had ripped one of her turrets apart as if she were a tin can being opened by a particularly sharp tin-opener. That caused her to turn away and face what she might have thought were lesser and not so powerful enemies. But there was no escape. Shells continued to batter her from all sides. Everywhere there were great gleaming silver scars on her paintwork where they had slammed into her. Her deck was a shambles, with debris and wreckage every-where, and angry little flames were begin-ning to erupt on all sides.

Desperately Lutjens ordered smoke. But the smoke screen had hardly commenced when, for some reason, it vanished once more leaving the dying ship naked to its enemies. Again shell after shell slammed mercilessly into the *Bismarck*. It was now almost as if the Tommies were using her as target practice, the broken Admiral told himself.

The crew's morale started to break at last. A stoker, his nerve gone, ran crazily through the explosions across the debris-strewn deck, heading for the bridge, shrieking, 'You're mad ... you're all mad ... stop for—' The exploding shell caught him in mid-

stride. His blood splattered on the buckled steel plates in great crimson gobs. He felt his bones breaking, urine and excreta streaming down his legs. For one second his contorted young face softened and a horrified Lutjens thought the rating was smiling up at him wearily. A moment later his severed head, encased in his steel helmet, rolled away and vanished into the scuppers.

Now the *Bismarck*, her rudders gone, was drifting aimlessly round and round, trailing thick black smoke behind her, the fire of her guns weakening by the instant, her life spluttering away in the ineffectual cannon fire of her shattered turrets. As the *Rodney* continued pounding her, great white columns of water rose nearly two hundred feet into the sky. Salvoes of that kind would have broken the back of the average destroyer and sunk her like a brick if she had steamed through one of them. Still, somehow, the *Bismarck* hung on. But not for long.

'Prepare the ship for sinking.' The order now went out. It was the last that anyone would receive from Admiral Lutjens. It seemed that he was no longer capable of making any constructive suggestions that might save the survivors. He was intent on going down with his ship. The men would have to look after themselves the best they could.

The engineer officers lit up the lower deck. Now there were brilliant lamps everywhere, illuminating the stark horror of the dying battleship: the shattered, crushed doors, the bulging split plates, the smoke gushing out everywhere, the dead lying abandoned. And men, hundreds of men, milling around stupidly. They had thrown away their combat gear and flash equipment. Now they were prepared for the ordeal in the arctic water that was to come, wearing inflated life-jackets and gas masks in preparation for the seawater hitting the electric motors and releasing their killing gases.

The *Bismarck* was sinking now. Lutjens had hidden himself. No one went to find him. They respected his wish to go down with his ship. Still there were those who felt he should have said something to the survivors. Instead Commander Gerhard Junack, the senior officer, present, barked, 'Don't give up hope, comrades. Be careful when interrogated by the enemy. *Sieg Heil.*'

The response was listless. The great days had already been forgotten. The men knew they were facing death or years of imprisonment. The old world had vanished.

Junack gave up. In a weary voice, he ordered, 'Abandon ship!'

It wasn't a moment too soon. By now the Tommies had shot out all the crippled giant's guns. They had left a smoking, lurching black ruin, which was clearly sinking. Tovey, feeling sickened at the sight, felt the ship was like a dog that had been run over. Someone had to put the dying beast down. He ordered his battleship to turn away. Next he had the cruiser *Dorsetshire* signalled. She was to sail in and finish the *Bismarck* off with her torpedoes. He was not going to risk his battleships in case the *Bismarck* had summoned up Doenitz's U-boats to torpedo them when they began to pick up survivors. But the head of the U-Boat Army had no such intention. His U-boats were spread across the French Atlantic coast waiting for the *Bismarck* to lead the Tommies into the trap. Now that the *Bismarck* wouldn't be coming, he didn't have the time to alter his dispositions. At least that's what he said later.

The survivors were hardly free of the ship when she keeled over to port. It was a frightening sight. Even those panicked sailors – splashing and slapping about in the freezing water as they tried to regain their breath – paused and stared momentarily, awed and strangely calm.

There was a frightening squeaking and groaning. The *Bismarck* was in its death throes. Later a handful of the survivors swore they heard the screams, the pleas, the curses of the men who were still trapped at that moment, as they realised they were going to their doom.

A magazine exploded. Five hundred yards away the awed matelots of the *Dorsetshire* felt the shock, as if someone had just punched them in the guts. Majestically the *Bismarck* rose slowly into the air. Higher and higher. For what seemed an age that great steel tomb paused there. Then slowly, inexorably, she started to slide beneath the waves. They leapt up to receive her greedily, only to recoil hissing and spluttering furiously, as they felt the searing heat of her boilers.

On the bridge of the *Dorsetshire*, shocked and ashen-faced, the officers stiffened to attention without a command being given. They felt no sense of triumph at the end of this great ship, only one of loss. As one, they raised their right hands to the brims of their caps in salute – the final tribute from the victors. Then with one last wild tumult of water, the *Bismarck* was gone.

The *Devonshire* steamed on to where the handful of survivors bobbed up and down in the oil slick. Not for long. A signal was coming through that U-boat periscopes had been sighted. Later it was reported that it was a false alarm, but that was later. So the cruiser steamed on, leaving the ocean silent and empty now, save for the mass of floating debris – and the one German on the rubber float, drifting aimlessly and sobbing, sobbing, sobbing, as if his very heart would break...

The Savage Conclusion

The smell of defeat was in the air that May afternoon, nearly sixty years ago now. Even the cool, fresh breeze coming in from the Baltic couldn't blow it away. The smell had settled on Wismar like a dreary grey dust. Now the port, which he had last seen four years before, lay in ruins, peopled by grey skeletons carrying their pathetic bits and pieces behind them in little wooden carts. Everywhere, there were demobilised veterans of the defeated *Wehrmacht* in their shabby grey uniforms, begging for cigarettes at street corners or fighting bitterly for the wet butts the foreigners had tossed into the gutter. All was grey, save for the ruddy, healthy British soldiers – rifles over their shoulders – who strode down the bomb-shattered streets purposefully like creatures from another world.

Captain Savage tapped his driver on the shoulder and ordered, 'See if that road there, Jones, leads to the harbour.' His voice was stiff and awkward, for he was still recovering

from the throat wound he had received in the Channel in the winter.

Jones said, 'The Admiral's arriving by train from Hamburg at fourteen hundred hours. We don't want to miss him, sir.'

Savage forced a smile for the rating's sake. 'Any admiral who arrives by train, Jones, *ought* to be missed. Don't worry. I'll get you to the station in time. Just want to make a little sentimental journey.'

Jones wondered what kind of sentimental journey the boss wanted to make in this arsehole of a place, but he didn't comment on the matter. Officers were a funny lot at the best of times and everybody knew Savage's explosive temper. So he kept his mouth shut and concentrated on weaving in and out of the line of shabby, grey whores offering their services to the Tommies.

Now Savage started to recognise the odd place in which he had found himself after his escape from Wesertimke in what now seemed another age. But now, in place of the leather-helmeted Hun cops directing traffic were the hatchet-faced British MPs, the Redcaps. Standing there in the swirling grey dust, they urged the Army trucks to move on between the bombed harbour docks, daubed with the slogans of the defeated Nazi Empire, *'Better Dead than Red'*, *'Never Again 1918'*. And over and over again that defiant

'Victory or Siberia'.

Grimly Savage nodded to himself. These days 'Siberia' was just up the road where the lines of the Red Army commenced. That's why the Admiral was coming in. Their Lordships wanted to have a look-see at the former German Navy's resources, just in case the Russians got too uppity and decided on trouble. Churchill himself had ordered the check to be carried out. If there was ever going to be another war, Winnie had decided the Huns would be on our side.

Savage sighed. It was a crazy world, he told himself.

The jeep slowed down to avoid the scores of potholes, caused by the Brylcreem boys. There were beached wrecks everywhere, flying the white flag of surrender, with bored matelots in steel helmets guarding the German ships. Savage knew he should shout at them and order them to get their 'fingers out'. But he wasn't really interested in naval discipline this afternoon. He had come here in the hope that he might still find her, though after four weeks in a defeated Germany and four years after they had parted, he hadn't much hope of doing so.

'Naturally, Harding,' he explained, as he sat bolt upright in his wheelchair, surrounded by his medicines and 'bloody pisspots', as he

282

called the nursing home's plastic bedpans, looking weaker now than the first time I had gone to hear his story, 'I'd tried the usual agencies of the time, UNRRA, Military Government, the Swiss Red Cross ... but nobody really seemed much interested in the poor Poles.' He had flashed me one of those bitter looks of his, but I thought most of the fire had gone. Vice-Admiral Horatio Savage, I told myself, was beginning to fade.

The jeep turned the corner. Before Savage lay the naval harbour, filled from end to end with wrecks, some deep in the water so that only their funnels and masts were visible. Others had been tossed over on their sides like children's toys by the blast of the RAF bombs. One or two were beached in the shallows, as if they were stranded metallic whales.

Then he saw her. Her deck was pocked with bomb shrapnel marks like the symptoms of some hideous, loathsome skin disease and she was listing to the water around her, blue and greasy with oil. 'Get closer, Jones,' Savage ordered, noting an odd tingling, electric feeling in his hands and a sudden shortness of breath. He was getting excited, too bloody soon, he told himself, as the rating manoeuvred his way the best he could towards the wreck.

* * *

'It was the *Kolding* all right, Harding, you know the old Danish tub, which was going to smuggle us to Sweden.' Savage paused, as if he was thinking how different his life might have been if the *Kolding* hadn't been hit. Perhaps, he wouldn't have been here, a lonely dying old man, surrounded by medicines and 'bloody pisspots', if he and Elena had have made it.

I looked at the old man. His face revealed little but there was a wet sheen to his faded eyes. I felt embarrassed for him. I looked away, out of the window.

Outside a hearse had drawn up. Two men in black suits were leaning against the big old Bells smoking discreetly, with their cigarettes cupped in their hands. Another of Mrs Hakewell-Smythe's 'clients' had gone the way of all flesh.

Savage saw me looking out of the window and said in that old bitter fashion of his, 'The harlot' – he presumably meant the owner of the 'Hollies' – 'always says, the finger had writ and passed on.' He snorted impatiently. 'The sooner it does me, the better. Then I'm out of here.'

'Don't say that, sir,' I tried to appease him. 'You have years left, and besides, I want to get your whole story down. You can't snuff it on me – *yet*.'

He obviously liked that, for he forgot about the funeral outside and said, 'It was the *Kolding* to which the traitor had taken us from the *Hein Muck* pub, which had gone in the bombing, too, I found out later, Harding. So once again, I had come to a dead end – or so I thought.' He paused as if he were trying to recall the full details of that May day so long ago, before he attempted to relate them to me. 'It was then that I met the Hun.'

I thought it better not to interrupt and ask which 'Hun'.

'He looked like an ex-officer, naval type, I suppose. Obviously down on his luck, poor bugger. Ankle-length overcoat devoid of badges of rank, concealing a missing leg. Instead he had a peg-leg and crutches. As you know, Harding, I don't go much on the Hun, but I felt sorry for this chap. Looked like a gentleman.'

On any occasion I would have laughed at the description. Who talks like that these days? Who's a gentleman for that matter? I'm not, for sure. But I let him carry on, feeling we were progressing now. For, although I was not particularly interested in the Polish girl – she was obviously long dead in 1945 – I *was* keen to learn more about Gestapo Müller, Eichmann's boss. I'd checked with the

German authority concerned with finding missing war criminals in Ludwigsburg and, of course, the Simon Wiesenthal Center in L.A. There Gestapo Müller, if he were still alive, was still number one on their list of most wanted war criminals.

'Yes?' Savage had demanded coldly – after all it was forbidden to talk to Germans except in the line of duty. 'What is it?'

The German's pale, half-starved face flushed a little, but he was no longer in a position to be proud as he had once been as the second-in-command of the *Prinz Eugen*. 'I saw you looking at the wreck of the *Kolding*,' he said in very good English. 'I was here in 1941, waiting for my ship when she was sunk.'

That got Savage. He reached in his pocket and brought a round tin of Capstan out. Offering it to the flushed German, he said, 'Take a handful for yourself.' The officer hesitated and Savage urged, 'Go on. I've still got plenty from last month's NAAFI ration.'

Whether or not the German knew what Savage meant by NAAFI ration was not clear, but he couldn't resist the temptation of the cigarettes, the only valid currency in Germany that year. He took a handful, trying not to be greedy and bowing his thanks as he did so. 'I can pay,' he began.

Savage cut him short. 'Don't think about it, please.'

Jones's eyes widened at that 'please'. The old man hated the Jerries like poison; now he was saying 'please' to one of them. Wonders would never cease.

'That's how I came to meet *Herr Kapitanleutnant* Jensen. He had his leg cut off by a bloke he called the "Pox Doctor" during the *Bismarck* business. Not a bad bloke for a Hun. Indeed we corresponded for a couple of years before he snuffed it.' Savage sniffed at the memory for some reason known only to himself.

Outside Mrs Hakewill-Smythe was saying, 'Please don't take the body past the front door, gentlemen. I don't want my clients to know that people die here ... And oh, by the way, if you have a replacement for her, there's a hundred in it for you as long as she or he only lasts a couple of months.'

I didn't comment. Instead to keep the momentum going, I said hastily, 'And it was this Jensen who led you to Gestapo Müller?'

'In a way, Harding. I thought if I could find him, he'd give me a clue – even if I had to beat it out of him personally – to what had happened to Elena.'

'And he did?'

'Yes, in a way,' Suddenly there was a note

of resignation in the old sailor's voice, as if he were realising for the first time that he was coming to the end of his story and that he had known all along that it was going to be an unhappy one.

Somehow or other, and it had involved a lot of wire-pulling, even a few threats, Savage and his new naval assistant on German Naval Matters, Unit 30 (a unit that would never be found in the Royal Navy's Order-of-Battle) arrived in the British sector of occupied Berlin.

Berlin was worse than Wismar: a sea of ruins, occupied now by the soldiers of four victorious allied armies, with their officials trying to restore some sort of order to a capital that had been under the Red Army's siege for nearly a month. All the same, Jensen, now in British battledress with a self-designed flash on the sleeve proclaiming he was a petty officer in German Naval Matters, Unit 30, was very resourceful. Plentifully supplied with packets of NAAFI fags for bribes, he greased the wheels everywhere, making Savage's task much easier.

'You know, Jensen was more like one of us, Harding. Not a bit like the typical Hun,' he confessed, as we sat there, listening to the sound of the departing hearse and the normal cackle of the demented old ladies below. 'If I hadn't have known he was a Hun,

I would have taken him for one of my own staff. What?'

'What,' I agreed and left it at that.

Over the month or so that Savage managed to wangle in Berlin, Jensen did his best to follow Gestapo Müller's trail through Berlin in the last days of the war: from his post in Hitler's bunker, the couple of days he had spent in Eichmann's hide-out in a cellar-shelter beneath the Kurfurstenstrasse until his apparent final disappearance, once the allied secret services had commenced asking about the man who knew more about German counter-espionage – especially against the Russians – in World War Two than any other.

For a while, the trail had gone dead, and Savage had gone into a black mood. Then Jensen had struck lucky. He had hobbled into the lobby of the senior officers' mess, which Savage was using as his HQ, announced by the club steward and, when the latter had been out of earshot, he whispered excitedly, 'They've found him, sir.'

Savage's black mood had vanished in an instant. 'Gestapo Müller? Where, man, don't waste time. Let me get my hands on the bastard ... I'll get the truth out...' The words had trailed away when he had recognised the look on the crippled German officer's face and he had said in a subdued tone, 'All right,

Jensen, tell me.'

Jensen, who by now knew the reason for this British officer's long search, said softly, 'In a grave in the old Jewish Cemetery in *Berlin-Mittel*. Apparently one of the grave units, employed by the Russians, buried his corpse there last week.' His voice faltered, 'Sorry, sir, I couldn't bring you something—'

Savage wasn't listening. He signalled to the nearest steward, 'Double whisky for two.'

The white-jacketed waiter looked as if he were about protest that Jensen was a German, but Savage didn't give him a chance. 'You heard me,' he snapped. 'Look sharp now!'

The waiter looked sharp...

'It was one of the worst days of my life,' Savage said softly, his gaze far away as he recalled the scene at the makeshift grave in the old Jewish cemetery, where ironically enough they had apparently buried that arch anti-semite Gestapo Müller. 'It is not something I care to recall, Harding, but it's seared on to my mind indelibly.'

I said nothing. I waited instead, realising yet again how much he felt.

'Jensen had found some poor old Hun pathologist down on his luck. He was making a living, so Jensen said, as an "angel maker".' He saw I didn't understand and added quickly, 'Abortionist, getting rid of unwanted babies. But Jensen had offered him two tins of Woodbines to have a dekko at the body to make sure that it was Gestapo Müller's. Naturally I was praying it might give us some clue to the whereabouts of Elena. A long shot, I know, but that was what I was hoping, while the grave-diggers toiled away by the light of Jensen's lantern. And I was right. It didn't disappoint us. It gave us *more* than a clue sadly.'

The sad-faced doctor sighed like a man who was sorely troubled. He looked up from the mess of clothing, uniform and human parts spread across the freshly disturbed soil, while the grave-diggers watched patiently, leaning on their shovels and sipping the 'Bass Best Pale Ale', again supplied courtesy of the NAAFI.

All was silent now in Central Berlin. The curfew was in place and all of them, save Savage and Jones risked being arrested for breaking it if the Russians caught them. But that didn't seem to bother them, German and British – they were too interested to hear the broken-down pathologist, who was now wiping his dirty hands on his patched *Wehrmacht* trousers before he commenced his statement, which Jensen would translate.

Savage puffed at his cigarette, the end glowing in the early autumn darkness. It had been a long search. As eager as he was to hear what the 'sawbones' had to say, he could wait a few minutes more now.

The doctor cleared his throat. It was an unpleasant sound and, to Savage, it didn't seem healthy; perhaps the German doctor needed to see a doctor himself. Finally he started to explain his findings and Jensen attempted to do his best, his face worried in the yellow light of the lantern, as he tried to translate the difficult forensic medical terms. 'There is some – er – putrefaction and the maggots have obscured the details of the wounds, which look a couple of months old. If I had a – er – lysol bath to kill the maggots, I could tell you more. 'He shrugged his painfully thin shoulders. 'But I haven't. However, it is clear that all three of them died violently.'

'*Three*?' Savage exclaimed sharply.

'Yes,' the pathologist, whom Jensen called the 'Pox Doctor', looked surprised. 'I said three,' he added in English, while Savage looked at him in the wavering light of the lantern, open-mouthed with surprise like some half-witted village yokel. He nodded to Jensen and the latter brought the lantern closer, as the doctor drew back the tarpaulin from the exhumed grave. 'You see – a very shallow burial,' he went on, as Jensen translated. 'The bodies disintegrated more as we scooped them out. But they are definitely the parts of three bodies.'

'Gestapo Müller – in three parts,' Savage said, totally bewildered as he stared at the bloody remains, alive with maggots.

The pathologist smiled cynically and said something quickly to Jensen. The latter hesitated. 'A lot of people like Müller have wanted to disappear these last few months – like taking a dive in a U-boat, we call it. He left some identification papers in the grave and that was that. Perhaps he's in South America already, for all I know.'

'And they are all people in their mid-twenties,' the pathologist added in German, as if he had understood Jensen's explanation. 'A quarter of a century younger than Müller, who is – was – forty-five. As old as the century.' He laughed hoarsely.

In the silence, Jensen held the lantern closer so that Savage could get a better look at the three corpses, or what was left of them. 'All are headless, sir, you see,' he said softly, as if he realised what this discovery meant to his new master. 'You can see he was making it harder to identify them and cover up his tracks. He probably bribed the graves commission man to "find" him here like this.'

Savage nodded his understanding.

'I did find something, however,' the

pathologist broke the heavy silence.

Savage looked up, but he wasn't interested now. Another trail to Elena had ended nowhere. 'On the woman,' he added in English.

Jensen looked sharply at his old shipmate. 'The woman?' he queried in English for Savage's benefit. He could see just how low the Tommy was.

'Yes, this one is a woman,' the 'Pox Doctor' replied in the same language and then in German. 'Her abdomen has not been subjected to the blowflies which lay the maggot eggs. So it is relatively intact.' He bent down to the middle piece of 'flesh' (that was the only way that a horrified, repelled Jensen could think of the three corpses) and with his bare hand he wiped away the soil caused by the grave-diggers. 'You see the vagina. Still intact. The legs are slightly spread, as you can observe, and I'm guessing but I think she had had sexual intercourse before she died so violently.'

The 'Pox Doctor' wiped his hands once again and reached into the pocket of his shabby tunic. 'This is interesting. It's in Polish. But you know me and foreign tongues—'

Savage cut in. 'Let me see that,' he ordered harshly.

Obediently the 'Pox Doctor' dropped the

294

dusty amulet into Savage's outstretched palm, as Jensen brought the flickering lantern closer. Hastily Savage blew off the remaining dirt and held it to the yellow light. The others waited tensely, wondering why the Tommy seemed to become so tense about a piece of enamel, cheap at that, with a Polack inscription on it.

Time passed leadenly. Still they waited. The Englishman seemed transfixed, staring at the object, suspended from a silver-plated chain, also cheap, as if he were hypnotised by it.

Jensen cleared his throat finally and asked, 'Is it important, Captain Savage?'

But Savage couldn't answer. His mind and memory were a million miles away. That night in the old crone's barn when he had first made love to her, she had told him about the amulet which she had worn around her neck and the picture it had contained. It had been given to her by her mother before the Germans had taken her from Warsaw. The portrait, cheap and crude, had been that of the Black Virgin of Cracow. Her mother had ordered her to keep it on her body, always; it would bring her luck and keep her out of harm's way.

That night, lying naked for the first time and feasting his eyes on Elena's young nubile body, he had spotted it resting between her breasts, where she had hidden it before the brutal German searches. 'It brings luck,' she had whispered lovingly.

Then he had bent down and kissed the nipple of each beautiful breast, replying in whispers, too, in case the old crone heard, 'From now on, Elena, I bring you luck. *Verstanden?*'

'*Verstanden*,' she had agreed and then they had made intense, passionate love.

Now she was a headless corpse. Savage swallowed hard and the tears welled up, hot and blinding, in his eyes.

Jensen saw them. Gently he took Savage's arm. 'I think it is better we go. It is long past curfew. We want no trouble, Captain Savage, do we?'

Numbly, Savage nodded. Jensen took his hand, holding his lantern high so that the Englishman could see his way out of the shattered old Jewish cemetery. Obediently, like a chastened, hurt child, the one-time 'Hun eater' allowed himself to be led. A few moments later they had disappeared into the silent night, broken only by the grunts of the grave-diggers, as they returned the soil over the body of Elena and her comrades in death ... It was all over.

Author's Note

At that last meeting, I promised Vice-Admiral Savage that I would look into the matter of Gestapo Müller's grave more thoroughly when I went to Germany. I did. The officials of the section of the Bavarian State Ministry concerned were, as usual, very helpful, exceedingly so. One wonders how a similar British department would have reacted if I had to come to them, enquiring about a supposedly long-dead British war criminal.

They knew about the first grave in the old Jewish cemetery and about the second one, also in Berlin, which bears the legend, 'To our dear papa ... from his children.' It has also been excavated *twice*. Naturally it does not contain the remains of our 'dear Papa'. So where is Gestapo Müller?

According to the Bavarian officials, Gestapo Müller – the head of that dreaded organisation which was feared throughout Europe for years in the 1930s and 1940s – was forgotten for years after the preliminary enquiries about his fate in the immediate post-war years. Then in the late sixties, two Mossad agents were arrested trying to break into his 'widow's' flat in Munich while she was in hospital. Thereafter the rumours started once more.

Gestapo Müller was spotted alive in many places, from Albania to the Argentina. Once more he became Germany's most wanted war criminal; and even today though he would be a hundred years old, he still heads the Bavarian Agency's list of wanted men. But where did he go? One of the officials, who shall remain nameless, took me aside after I had surveyed the relevant documents and like two old 'queens' sizing each up in the lavatories, he told me – 'unofficially' of course – what the Bavarians thought.

'It was the CIA of course. They had spread the rumour that he had gone over to the Russians in '45. In reality he had worked for them against the "Ivans" and then they had smuggled him out through Switzerland to the States and Langley. Here he was promoted to the rank of general, worked for them as Europe's top expert on Russian spy networks before he retired with a new family, American, somewhere in the wilds of West Virginia.'

I accepted all this without blinking an eyelid. (Obviously my informant in the Bavarian

WC had never been to the 'wilds of West Virginia.' I nodded in agreement, as he concluded with, 'Typical *Ami*, you know, Herr Harding. A very devious people, the Americans. I wouldn't trust them as far as I could throw them, *nicht wahr*.'

Nicht wahr, indeed!

I was going to call Savage immediately when I got back with my news. But it was too late. Instead there was a letter waiting for me which would have made the call and a journey to the 'Hollies' unnecessary.

It wasn't much of a letter. For the envelope contained a poor, blurred photograph. It was obviously an amateurish effort. Later I discovered it had been taken by no less than Mrs Hakewill-Smythe.

Even Mrs Hakewill-Smythe's cheap snap could not conceal the tawdriness of the 'naval' funeral, as she called it: a squad of boys from the local Sea Scouts, a Marine bugler and a portly old boy from the Royal Naval Association, heavy with polished medals, but looking either drunk or confused (perhaps both) in the standard brass-buttoned blazer and beret.

'We did him proud,' Mrs Hakewill-Smythe gushed in her accompanying note. 'It was a real naval send-off for a brave navy man. There must have been at least half a dozen of my clients from the home present at the ceremony and the *Gazette* did him proud, a whole half column. They would have sent a photographer, but there'd been an accident on the by-pass and naturally the paper needed him out there that morning...'

I put down the note and thought to myself, what can one do? Grin and bear it? I suppose Savage would have said in his wartime slang that he still affected all those years later, 'Roll on death and let's have a go at the angels.' Who bloody well knows?

So he had died: Vice-Admiral Horatio Savage, DSC, MC, a sailor who had fought at Dunkirk, escaped from Wesertimke, been wounded at Walcheren ... and endured it all stoically to live into our own Brave New World.

Today, a year after the Admiral's death, all I can do is quote that last line from Fitzgerald's *Great Gatsby*. It seems apt enough. 'So we beat on, boats against the current, borne back ceaselessly into the past...'